The Alpha Decade Book

A celebration of ten years of Alpha writing
Written by members of

Alpha Writers Group

Copyright © 2016 Alpha Writers Group

All rights reserved. Any unauthorised broadcasting, public performance, copying or recording will constitute an infringement of copyright. No part of this book may be reproduced or transmitted in any form or by any means, electronically or mechanical, including photocopying, fax, data transmittal, internet site, recording or any information storage or retrieval system without the express written permission of the publisher except for the use of brief quotations in a book review.

Printed in the United Kingdom

First Printing, 2016 Alfie Dog Limited

The author can be found at: authors@alfiedog.com

ISBN 978-1-909894-31-0

Published by
Alfie Dog Limited
Schilde Lodge, Tholthorpe,
North Yorkshire, YO61 1SN
Tel: 0207 193 33 90

DEDICATION

"You only learn to be a better writer by actually writing."
Doris Lessing.

"Writing is an adventure."
Winston Churchill.

The Alpha Decade Book is the story of how The Alpha Group of Writers was formed, and how our members shared the exciting adventure of trying to become better writers.

To celebrate the first decade of Alpha Writers our members have selected a vibrant medley of stories – old and new – to illustrate our progress over the ten Alpha Seasons.

The email-based group is the brainchild of **Olaf Chedzoy.**

In May 2004 Olaf published a letter in Writers' News asking potential members to contact him.

The first meeting of Alpha Writers – eighteen members in all – took place in cyberspace on Thursday the 16th of September 2004.

One decade later we'd totalled 130 virtual meetings and fixed the date for the start of Alpha Season XI.

This book is first of all dedicated to **Olaf** for his untiring encouragement and occasional hectoring which has shaped Alpha Writers into what we are today and stimulated us to continue the never-ending quest for excellence in writing.

A huge bouquet of accolades goes to the many Alpha members – past and present – whose enthusiasm for all aspects of writing made this decade an enjoyable adventure for us all.

CONTENTS

Season I – 2004 - 2005	1
An Important Decision – Rosemary	5
Season II – 2005 - 2006	20
Rounded with Snow - Zena	23
Season III 2006 - 2007	27
The Purple Dress – Sally	29
Season IV – 2007 - 2008	35
First Day at Big School - Suzanne	38
Season V – 2008 – 2009	43
A Cold Day in Hell – Chris	45
Season VI – 2009 – 2010	54
Spring Symphony – Christine	57
Season VII – 2010 – 2011	67
The Crossing – Morgen	69
Season VIII – 2011 – 2012	82
Victorian Railways – Olaf	85
Season IX – 2012 – 2013	93
The Rundle Ruins – Rose	95
Season X – 2013 - 2014	105
It's Time – Geoff	108

Both our readers and authors cover many countries. Therefore, it is our policy not to standardise spellings or punctuation marks, but to leave them to reflect the voice of the author. After all, who's to say we would be right on the choice we made? It is part of the fascinating challenge of reading, to open a window onto how language has changed through separated usage.

ALPHA SEASON I.
2004-2005

Action...

The first Alphaday arrived and around the world 18 PCs were switched on in breathless expectation of what was forthcoming.

Olaf issued a calendar for the season consisting of 13 Alphadays: all Thursdays at 3-weekly intervals. Each Alphaday had an agenda of tasks and activities.

Our common passion was writing and the item on the agenda that gave us all itchy fingers was then, and still is, The Challenge.

Olaf set a new challenge every Alphaday. We scribbled. Olaf collected our entries and sent them off to an external judge for assessment. He managed to find professional writers for most of them.

Other items on that first season's agenda were regular discussions on themes suggested by Olaf. The replies were both insightful and thought-provoking.

There was also a longitudinal exercise: a story which was alternately reduced and extended... like Chinese whispers.

Margaret (featured below) had the excellent idea of sending out an Alpha Writers' Log every Alphaday. She collected information about our writing activities outside the Alpha cocoon. As a result, we discovered that we had two professional garden writers, a genealogist, a marketing tutor, an educational columnist, and many a novelist looking for a publisher.

The biggest feat of all was our group novella, *The Scribeham Chronicle*. Olaf provided the setting, the characters and notes to direct the plot. He also wrote a prologue and an epilogue and somehow the story hung together... not perfectly, but very engagingly.

Background...
Our group was made up of writers who for some reason couldn't attend a conventional writers' group. Work, dependent relatives and other reasons were mentioned, and then there were those who lived overseas.

From the beginning we prided ourselves on our cosmopolitan element. We had members from the Turks and Caicos Islands, from Saudi Arabia, Germany and France. Over the years we've covered most of the continents and it's been a fantastic asset for the group.

Conflict...
Our group is like a writers' microcosm. Our challenges mimic the battle for winning a publishing deal. It's on a small scale and done in a friendly, fun atmosphere, but we enjoy the competitive aspect.

Writers do have vulnerable egos and it hurts when a challenge entry is not appreciated... however much we may try to hide such feelings. And the sense of jubilation experienced by a winner is – let's be honest – quite out of proportion with the modest dimensions of our intimate little group. Still, conflict is the substance of drama, and we love it.

Dénouement...
It was an exciting year; in many ways it was a glamorous year. Most of us had joined without any preconceived idea of what we expected. We simply waited for Olaf to tell us what to do.

Olaf planned, programmed, prepared and canvassed tirelessly in order to make the Alpha experiment a success. There were times when things came a bit unstuck, but they got mended.

Olaf had persuaded Jonathan Telfer, editor of Writers' News, to give us plenty of coverage in the magazine. Alpha members enjoyed the privilege of a monthly slot where we took it in turns to write about our experience – complete with photo!

Ending...
We'd given the Alpha experiment our best. We'd found a group with one shared passion: Writing. We'd bonded inside the group and we were keen to continue what we'd started so auspiciously.

Here's how Zena summed it up for Writers' News Magazine:

> *The group's last challenge was to write the first page of a crime / whodunit novel. To judge the contributions Olaf secured the assistance of the internationally famous crime writer,* Andrew Taylor, *whose comments about the high standard of entries made Zena proud of the group's achievements.*

> *"The final challenge set and judged, the last bulletins sent out to members, and our online Alpha year draws to a close," she says. "Has it been a success? Undoubtedly," she*

says. *"A spur to write more and better? Without question. Time well spent? Oh, Yes, indeed yes."*

The sample challenge we've chosen from Season I is, of course, the one mentioned above:

Alpha Season I, Challenge 10:

'Write the first page of a crime/whodunit type of novel, with 250-300 words. You do not need a synopsis – you don't even need to have any idea how it ends or even what happens on page 2 – but you do need a 'hook' in the first paragraph, and you need to add to it later in the page so the reader will want to turn to the next page.'

The winning entry, written by Margaret:
"So, dearie, you're the creep everyone's afraid of?" Florence sneered as she studied the sketch under the street lamp.

Empty eyes stared back at her. Icy eyes. Like death itself, Florence thought. She liked that idea. The picture of a murderer. Dead eyes.

She let out a guffaw and watched her nicotine-yellow breath weave round the paper. The hazy glow from the light etched a halo-like shadow on to the man's forehead. Florence smiled, then blew a kiss to him, before stuffing the drawing into her handbag.

Some said she was too old for the game. And the younger girls sniggered at her behind her back. Let them laugh. They were the ones cowered in corners and huddled in packs now there was a murderer loose.

"Not me loveys," she said aloud. She'd been in the business twenty years. Nothing much bothered her these days. She was surprised that the thought saddened her.

Florence caressed the scar, snaking along her cheek, as a new girl hurried towards her. The girl, who called herself Celeste, reeled from side to side in her turquoise stilettos. Innocence gleamed from Celeste's satin complexion. She clasped her hands together. Her fingers were long, the nails painted a soft peach.

As she drew closer, Florence sniffed. Lavender. Celeste always reeked of bloody lavender. Tonight there was something else wafting between them – the pungent odour of fear.

"Can I stick with you tonight, Flo?" Celeste stuttered. "I mean, you know, with that madman roaming the streets?"

Florence smirked. "Course you can, lovey." She teased her tongue over her flame-red lipstick. It was going to be a good night.

The Alpha Decade contribution vaguely inspired by the Season I brief:

An Important Decision
Written by Rosemary.

"I can't believe that this time tomorrow we'll be on a beach in Spain," said Marcie bouncing up and down as she spoke. She was literally tingling with excitement. "It'll be our first foreign holiday together."

Gary sneered at her. "Hello, my name's Marcie and my specialist subject is stating the bleedin' obvious."

Marcie stopped bouncing. "There's no need to be like that, Gary. I know you've been abroad a lot, but I haven't." It had been his worldly wisdom which had first made her notice him. Somehow it made him seem so cool next to the other blokes she met. That and his cheeky smile, though she didn't seem to see so much of that these days.

"Yeah, well. Just go downstairs out of me way while I pack. You don't want me to forget summat do you?"

Marcie thought he was leering rather than grinning. It gave her an uneasy feeling. She shivered slightly, remembering the look he'd given her when she gave him the parcel she'd picked up from his mate Gavin's kid brother the week before.

"I'll make us a cup o' tea." She almost danced down the stairs recovering some of her mood by thinking of drinking sangria overlooking the sea. She'd been to Spain once before on a family holiday about 12 years ago. She must have been about 10, but it was the best holiday she could ever remember. Even so, going away with Gary, her very own boyfriend was going to be way better.

They'd only moved in together the previous month, but Marcie was certain that Gary was THE one, despite everything her mother had said. Of course now her mum was on her own she was bound to worry about her little girl. The kettle belched steam like an overenthusiastic dragon and she pressed the faulty rocker switch to stop it.

She went back upstairs carrying two mugs of steaming tea and gently pushed the bedroom door open with her back. Suddenly it slammed shut again and the scalding tea spilt down her wrists.

"I told you to stay downstairs, you stupid cow."

Marcie bit her bottom lip as she felt a heaving sob rise up from nowhere. Gary needed this holiday so much. He'd been working all hours, often going back in the evening. She told herself it was the pressure and it wasn't his fault as she went down to the kitchen to run her hands under the cold water. Money had been so tight recently, she knew he was worried. He hadn't meant to do it, any more than he'd meant to hit her the night he came back from Gavin's, drunk. It would all be different when they were away together.

"Two of you travelling?"

Marcie handed their tickets to the check-in lady at the airport desk, and grinned at Gary.

"Did you pack the bags yourself?"

"Yes," she said as Gary stood looking around the terminal behind them.

"And are you carrying any of these items?" The check-in clerk indicated the picture symbols attached to the front of the counter.

"No," Marcie said, then hesitated a moment. She had no idea what Gary had packed and he wasn't taking any notice at all. She chided herself for being ridiculous and smiled at the lady.

She took their boarding cards and they headed through to Departures. She could feel the butterflies in her stomach and when Gary suggested they get a drink it seemed like a great idea to steady her nerves. She gazed in the windows of the stores as they passed, wishing she could do more than window shop.

It didn't seem like five minutes before they'd landed at the other end and were trying to pull their bags off the carousel onto the trolley.

"Here you push this, Marce," Gary instructed as they made their way through all the arrival processes.

"Why me?" She hated it when he abbreviated her name. He said it was endearment, but he always did it when he was ordering her about.

"Just do it," he said scowling at her.

Marcie thought how funny it was that when she walked

past customs officers she felt nervous even though she'd only got her holiday stuff. She relaxed when they came out into the Arrivals hall to find their holiday rep. Gary was smiling for the first time and she thought he was finally starting to relax.

She'd made sure she'd got one of those cheap phone packages for calling from abroad before they set off and while Gary went to find the gents, she rang her mate Jo to tell her they'd arrived. She would have rung her mum, but it was a bit late and she presumed her mum would have gone to bed. She was forgetting it was an hour earlier back home.

Where they were staying wasn't too far from the airport and they were one of the first drop offs. It was a self-catering place, basic but ok.

"I'm glad we're here. I'm tired after the travelling." Marcie kicked off her shoes and lugged her case onto the bed to unpack.

"Why don't you stay here, love, and I'll go and do a recce and then bring us back a pizza or summmat?"

Gary hardly ever called her 'love'. It was great to see the real Gary coming out. She always said he could be really considerate. "Thanks, Gary. I'll unpack then."

"I'll do mine," he snapped, taking her by surprise. He lifted his case into the corner and checked the lock. She frowned, but if he'd brought a present for her then she supposed it made sense.

She waited a couple of hours for him, but he didn't come back. He'd probably got talking to someone in the bar and lost track of time. She wasn't really hungry so in the end she went to bed. By the time she got up in the morning the sun was shining and Gary was snoring soundly. She had no idea what time he'd come in. She opened the shutters.

"What the hell are you doing?" Gary sat up suddenly. "Turn that bleeding light off, I'm trying to sleep here."

"I was only…"

"Well don't," he rolled over as she pulled the shutters back into place. She sighed heavily. It was decision time. She could either sit here as she did at home, or she could go out and enjoy the sunshine and find some breakfast. She could hear her mum's words echoing after Dad died. 'I'll be ok, love. I always made sure I could still do things on my own.' Marcie made a decision, her mum was right. It was her holiday too. She scribbled a note on the back of a flyer for jet ski hire and went out as quietly as she could, taking her stuff for the pool with her.

It was 4pm before Gary joined her. "Where've you been?" He looked annoyed.

"I had a walk round and then I've been here listening to my iPod." She pulled the earphone out of her ear. She'd only had one in so she could hear what was going on around the pool.

"Well I'm hungry. Let's get some food, my treat."

She shrugged. It had been a while since breakfast and she hadn't bothered with lunch. She gathered her belongings and followed him. With Gary it was no good suggesting they try any of the local food. That was never going to happen, so they settled themselves in a place selling good old English fry ups, alongside some local dishes. He ordered a litre of wine, so Marcie was surprised when he asked for a beer as well. She presumed he was planning to drink both. As the meal progressed he kept filling her glass and she was sure he was only drinking the beer, even though he'd put a little of the wine in his glass.

"Looks like we'd better get you back," he said and indicated he wanted the bill. She was stunned when he pulled his wallet out to pay and it was stuffed with notes. He'd told her to only get him €200 before they came. He must have gone to the cashpoint.

She staggered back to the apartment with Gary's help. She couldn't remember feeling quite this wobbly from alcohol before. She fell into bed and was out like a light. She woke up needing a drink of water a few hours later and was surprised to find she was on her own and Gary was nowhere about. It was too late to ring home and she really wasn't feeling great, so she went back to bed.

The next day started much the same. Gary was asleep where he should be and, despite the hangover, she wanted to go out. She hesitated, the holiday was so they could spend time together, but she didn't want to waste the whole day. She'd imagined they'd be going on trips out and lying by the pool together. She remembered some of the places they'd been to on the holiday when she was a kid. It made up her mind. She got her things together and went out. This time she got a bus to the next town and had a look round. She had breakfast in a place that had a sign saying it was available to rent. Not just rooms so people could stay there, the whole restaurant! She started to dream what it would be like to have her own taverna and what she'd do differently. Her mum had always worked in catering and having her own place had been her mum's dream when she was younger. Marcie rang her mum as she ate her breakfast.

"I've found us a great place to work, Mum." Her mum laughed as Marcie told her all about it. Marcie realised she was relaxed and really enjoying herself, even though Gary wasn't there.

She was back by the pool when he found her about 4.30pm. The pattern was much the same as the day before.

She didn't dare ask him where he'd been. She knew how he'd react. Then she had a thought. If he did it tonight, she'd follow him. They went back to the same café to eat. He ordered wine for her again, but she decided she wasn't going to drink much of it, but she needed him to think she had. Her chance came when he went off to the gents and she was able to tip most of it into the plant behind her. She ended up drinking only a couple of glasses, but the odd thing was she felt just as drunk.

He took her back to the apartment and she was asleep long before there was time for her to plan how to follow him. The pattern continued the following day. She caught the bus back to 'her taverna' and sat daydreaming. She even went as far as writing down the number of the agent from the sign. She knew she'd never do anything with it, but the lightness she felt, as she sat in the dappled sunshine imagining the changes she'd make to the menu, was something she'd almost forgotten.

Lying by the pool, she began to form a plan for the evening. The first part was to have a large late lunch so that she wouldn't be hungry.

When they sat down in their usual place she went through the motions of ordering both food and wine, but before it even arrived she was moving to the next stage of the plan.

"I don't feel very well."

"Should have stayed in bed like I did." Gary seemed quite pleased with himself, even though he wasn't seeing anything much of the resort by daylight.

"Maybe I've had too much sun." She made a point of mopping her forehead with the paper napkin and then headed for the ladies, wobbling slightly as she went.

By the time she got back the food was there and she

deliberately moved it around her plate without eating any.

"Here have a drink. It'll make you feel better," Gary said, filling her glass almost brim full with wine.

"I think I'll leave it thanks. Maybe I should go back and lie down. I'll wait till you finish."

"Yeah, I'll walk you back."

She couldn't believe that at no point in the week had Gary complained that she wasn't up to going out with him in the evenings. He'd not even made many snide remarks about her doing her own thing during the day. She had an uneasy feeling that something was wrong; very wrong.

Back at the apartment she stripped down to her tee shirt and climbed under the sheet that covered the bed.

"You don't need me here do you?" Gary didn't look as though he planned to stay even if she did say 'yes'.

"No, I'll see you later."

"Yeah, sleep well." And with that he'd gone. She heard some scuffling outside the apartment door. "It's ok, love, just dropped me wallet."

Marcie frowned. There it was again; 'love'. She listened to his steps going down to street level and then went to the window to see which way he headed, opening the shutters only far enough to allow her to see out. He'd headed to the town they were on the edge of. It would be impossible to follow him, but she could at least go out and say she felt better so she thought she'd join him, if she could find which bar he was in.

She dressed in more comfortable clothes than she'd normally wear for a night out. She didn't want to attract any unwelcome attention while she was looking for him and who knew how many bars she'd have to look in first? She picked up her bag, quickly ran a comb through her hair and headed for the door. She turned the handle and pulled it towards her. Nothing happened.

"What the…"

The door was locked. Gary had locked her in and taken the key with him. She was a prisoner. She pulled the door again. Perhaps the handle was stuck. Surely he wouldn't do that. Maybe he was doing it for her safety, but what if she had to get out in a hurry if there were a problem? She frowned deeply and sat on the edge of the bed. Gary had locked her in. Gary didn't want her to follow him. She shook her head. Surely she was wrong. She got up and tried the door again. Still nothing. She turned and saw Gary's still locked case in the corner of the room, the dials all carefully turned to zero. The way the week was going, it was very unlikely that it had a present for her in it. She looked at the four-digit combination. It was set to all the zeros. He wasn't likely to be back for hours. What numbers might he use? She tried the year he was born and then the day and month of his birthday. It didn't move. There was nothing else for it. She sat on the floor in front of the case and started with 0-0-0-1.

"Please, God, don't let it be 9-9-9-9." She turned it to that just in case. She laughed and went back to doing the numbers in turn. 0-2-3-1, 0-2-3-2. She slumped back against the wall. This could take all night. She looked at her watch, it was only 7pm. She'd probably got all night. An hour and a half later she was up to 2-4-5-3 and decided to ring Jo. Maybe if she talked to her friend she'd be able to make some sense of it all.

"Marcie, just come home. Get on the next flight out of there and come home."

"I can't. I've got no money and besides I can't get out of the apartment."

"Tomorrow then. I'll lend you the money."

"But it might all be ok."

"Marcie, will you listen to yourself? It is clearly not ok. Come home. Do you want me to ring your mum?"

"NO." Marcie almost shouted at her friend. "Sorry," she said more quietly. "It's just…" but she couldn't finish the sentence. What was it just? She didn't want her mum to know she was right? She didn't want to feel stupid? She wanted it all to be ok and there to be a reasonable explanation. "Look, Jo, I'll ring you tomorrow. I'll be ok, right."

2-4-5-4, 2-4-5-5.

She carried on for another hour or so, but by 10pm and having got to 5-7-4-7 she had still not opened the case. She reset it to the zeros and went to bed.

It was the fifth day of the holiday. Nothing much had changed. Marcie's tan was developing nicely and she had totally fallen in love with the neighbouring town. She had been trying to work out a plan for later that day when it came to her. Around 3pm she headed for the café that Gary had taken to going to and ordered both food and drink. She knew when he didn't find her by the pool he was likely to head there. The wine tasted good as she relaxed over her paella. She'd only ordered a small carafe and was just starting her second glass when she heard him.

"What are you doing here?"

"I was hungry and I thought this way you'd find me easily." She was trying to sound as charming as possible, but held her glass close, quickly pouring the remaining wine from the carafe. He sat opposite to her and clicked his fingers to attract attention. She hated when he did that.

"I thought I might come with you to the bar tonight," she tried to be casual. It was more than half way through the week and so far she hadn't been out past 8pm.

"Yeah, great," he said but from the way he was staring at the mini-skirted blonde going by in the street she knew he hadn't heard a word she'd said.

She sipped the wine slowly, watching him. Waiting for him to talk. He didn't.

"So where are we going?" she asked after an uncomfortably long silence.

"I thought you were ill," he said picking up a chip.

Slowly and patiently she said, "No, I'm fine."

"I'm meeting some of the lads to watch the football, you'll be bored."

"Right," she didn't know what to say to avoid a scene. "I'll just go back then shall I?"

"There's a good girl."

She could feel her cheeks flushing. This was not the holiday she'd had in mind. She looked at him closely. He wasn't even that good-looking. She wondered if she could go to the bar and meet someone else, but quickly dismissed that as she thought of his jealous rages.

She listened to his steps walking away from the apartment. Of course he'd walked her back again. She let the quiet continue for ten minutes and then got off the bed.

5-7-4-8, 5-7-4-9… 6-2-7-1, 6-2-7-2 she heard a slight click as the tumblers of the lock fell into place. Bingo.

Her heart was racing as she laid the case down flat and started to run the zip round the edge. She memorised the position the case had been in and that of the closed zip. She couldn't afford to take any chances. She was ready to open the lid. Her palms were sweating. What was she expecting to find? She had no idea but she certainly thought there was going to be something more than dirty underwear. She listened, but there was no sound outside. She lifted the lid and leant it back against the wall. Carefully laid across the top were jeans and beach shorts. She lifted the edge and gasped. Underneath was more money in euro bills than she'd ever seen in her life. She thought of the broken kettle and the times he'd shouted at her for spending too much. She frowned. She ran her hands round the case and felt a plastic bale. She moved things aside to get a closer look.

"Shit." She knew exactly what she was looking at. Well not exactly, obviously there were different types of white powder, but it certainly wasn't talc! And there was more than one. She gulped. Her hands were shaking as she started to put everything back into the case in exactly the same position she'd found it. She zipped the case and reset the lock to all the zeros then stood it in the corner where it had been before. She was cold and trembling as she went to the bathroom and threw up. She had brought the case into the country. It had been Marcie who pushed the trolley. Marcie who checked it in. Marcie who said she'd packed it herself. She retched again, but nothing more came up.

She wanted to go home. Not to the flat she shared with Gary, really home. To her mum's house. To the little bedroom with butterflies on the wallpaper. She'd promised to ring Jo, but what could she say? 'My boyfriend's a drug dealer and I'm terrified.' She needed a plan. She trusted Jo, they'd been mates since starting school. Jo would help. She sat with her head in her hands trying to think what to do next.

"Jo."

"Marcie, you all right? You sound different. Gary's not been knocking you about again has he?"

She could hear the anger in her friend's voice and it gave her courage. "No, nothing like that." She felt the tears start to fall as she began to tell Jo what had happened. "I need to turn him in, Jo, but I don't know what to do. Not here. I don't want to do it here."

"What if he's sold it all though?"

"I dunno. I hadn't thought of that. There's a lot."

Jo agreed to talk to the police at home and ask them what Marcie should do. Marcie sat fidgeting with a piece of paper. She wanted to write down what actions she needed to take, she was scared of losing the thoughts, but if Gary saw it there'd be real trouble. Most of all she had to stay calm and not let on that she knew anything. What was that saying that everyone seemed to put on mugs now 'Keep calm and carry on', yeah, that was it and it was exactly what she needed to do. She couldn't leave and go home early. She'd got to stay another two days and she'd have to meet up with Gary each afternoon or he'd be suspicious, or angry, or both! She wondered if she still loved him, but right now she was too numb to know. What if she turned him in and he came after her? Or his mates? What was she getting into?

She lay awake listening. She could hear drunken revelry outside the apartment, but strangely didn't want to be part of it. It was as though she had suddenly grown older and all this partying wasn't for her anymore. She needed a plan. What if…

She woke with a start. She could hear clattering around the apartment. Her heart was thumping. She didn't move. Then she heard the sound of a case zip opening. Gary, she presumed and breathed a little more deeply. She didn't want him to know she was awake. She steadied her breathing and hoped that her heart was not as loud as it sounded thudding in her ears. Eventually she heard him climb into bed next to her and shift position. She rolled onto her side and lay quietly in the darkness.

She lay by the pool the next day, groggy and catching up on the sleep she hadn't got the night before. Marcie jumped when her phone vibrated under her pillow.

"It's me, Jo, can you talk?" Jo was almost whispering as though there were people her end she didn't want to hear what she said. Marcie smiled to think of her friend being all conspiratorial in an otherwise empty house. Then she realised it was daytime so she was probably at work.

"Yeah, give me a minute." Marcie looked around. She hadn't got to know anyone, but for all she knew they might know Gary. She picked up her bag and started walking down the road towards the bus stop. "Ok."

"There'll be officers waiting at Heathrow to pick him up. You need to make sure he's got his own case and that you've got yours and nothing's been put in it. They'll pull you both in. Try to make it look as though they haven't been tipped off."

"Then what?"

"They'll let you go."

"But I can't go back to the flat." Marcie drew a breath in sharply. "Jo, I can't ever go back to the flat."

"Ok, we'll work something out. Anyway, the police want to talk to you too. Can I give them your number?"

They rang that afternoon not long before she was expecting Gary to arrive. She was sweating as they talked to her. "What? Can you say that again?"

"We'll need you to testify against him at the trial."

"I don't know. It won't be safe. I need to think."

"We'll call you again tomorrow."

"Make it early. Early morning will be good. It's not safe at this time of day. He's coming."

She hung up without waiting for a reply and slipped the phone into her pocket, hoping he hadn't seen.

She'd hired a car. Gary didn't need to know, and besides there were some places she wanted to check out before she went back. It was now the last full day and Marcie couldn't sleep. Gary hadn't been back long, but she waited until he was snoring before she got up.

Driving into the sunrise was always beautiful. To Marcie it signalled opportunity and anything being possible. Sure the mist hanging just above ground level was more than a little eerie, but nothing could be as bad as what she was leaving behind. Her mobile phone rang and she pulled off the road.

The greeting was brief; it was the call she'd been expecting. She took a deep breath and nodded to herself. "I need a safe flat and a new identity a long way from Sheffield, but yes, I'll testify." She let out a long breath and slumped in the seat as she hung up the call. It would all be over soon, and besides she'd made an appointment with the agent to view the taverna that was available to rent in the next town. This might just be the time to start a new life for herself and her mum.

ALPHA SEASON II.
2005-2006

Back to Basics...
Olaf had no more local, literary celebrities lined up to judge our challenges, and we decided to do it ourselves for Season II. We'd come to enjoy the buzz of having the proud winners held up for the group's admiration.

We needed a system. We tried some systems. It proved impossible to place entries in order of merit; there were too many equal winners. It took us over a year and many a heated debate to agree on our present system.

We needed criteria. The previous judges had used their own criteria and they were inevitably subjective. Could we define an objective set of criteria? We enumerated them all in different orders of preference: plot, spelling, style, grammar, tension, punctuation etc. Which of these were important? There were as many answers as there were members.

We're all different and our carefully considered priorities are... subjective.

The debate continues to surface every now and then.

Pioneering, Publicity, Publication...
There weren't many email only writers' groups. In 2005 Alpha Writers stood out as a pioneering venture.

Olaf worked tirelessly to promote the Alpha model so that others could benefit from our experience. He put together a book which recorded the first year of the Alpha experiment. He applied for, and obtained, a grant from The Arts Council which funded the publication of the first Alpha book:

Alpha Writers: The Birth of an email writing group.
It was self-published as a neat paperback in April 2006. The second part of the book, 80 pages and a total of 30,000 words, consisted of the group novella we'd written in Season I:

The Scribeham Chronicle.
It was the greatest single achievement of the group so far and we felt justly proud.

Writers' News published another piece by Olaf about the second Alpha season in which he described some of our challenges, as follows:

Phatic...
"Particularly notable was the idea of 'phatic' writing which David brought to my notice (and like most of you, I had never heard of it before). Phatic writing is a bit like pruning in reverse: i.e. inserting a passage which a story could well do without, although there is arguably a finer definition than that. I duly set a challenge to write a phatic passage to be inserted in one of my stories. Ten members submitted passages (all within the 300 word limit) all of which met the definition well, but were incredibly difficult to judge with Christine gaining a very narrow win.

Even more interesting was a challenge to write 300 words about 'very' – a word which has only emphasis, but no meaning.

For ingenuity, how many authors' names could you include in a 300-word passage which still makes sense when it is read

out? Geoff managed over 60, but he still didn't win!"
(From the article in Writers' News, June 2006.)

Another challenge from Season II had the following brief:

Alpha Season II, Challenge 6:

'**A holiday anecdote.** Pick out one positive experience from any holiday you've had, and present it as an item of interest which goes beyond anything the holiday promoters envisaged. (Praise for the hotel you stayed at wouldn't qualify unless there was something unusual.)
300 words.'

This entry from Christine was one of the winners:

Ready, steady... go!
I jump off the edge of the cliff. Eight hundred metres down is the tiny-looking strip of beach where we're supposed to land. I cling, white-knuckled, to the loop on the instructor's harness. "Relax," he orders. I obey and become aware of the serene peacefulness around me. The only sound is the gentle, reassuring swish of the hang-glider's wings.

I'm flying!

Rio de Janeiro is spread out below me, outlined by sea, mountains and forests. As we catch a thermal and veer round I look down on the dense, green canopy of the Floresta da Tijuca, the world's biggest urban forest and playground for groups of nimble macaque monkeys.

I can now see the vertical rock wall and the eroded carving of a face left by an ancient civilisation. Openings through the ears lead to a cave system, but no one knows what mystery is hidden there.

I'm carried by the soft, balmy air and nearer the city luxurious mansions nestle in forest clearings. Rich kids from these homes travel daily to prestigious schools in the family limousine with chauffeur and bodyguard to deter kidnappers.

Up and round on another thermal. On the horizon is a mountainside crowded with a spreading, sprawling, scrunched mass of makeshift houses. I point out the favela to my instructor who shrugs. Cariocas* are reluctant to discuss the subject. About 20% of Rio's population live in these favelas where poverty is rampant and drug-lords rule.

We're losing height. São Conrado beach appears. The next beach up is Leblon, with luxury shopping arcades and international hotels. Then Ipanema and Copacabana, cult centres for 'the body beautiful' and year-round sun worship.

I panic as the ground rushes up towards me... too fast. But my instructor is in control and we touch down safely.

Carioca: Native of Rio. Also used as an adjective.

The following Alpha Decade book contribution was inspired by the Season II brief:

Rounded with Snow
Written by Zena.

Early on the evening of 23rd December, we took the U-Bahn to the Weihnachtsmarkt in Stuttgart, one of Germany's oldest, which was lit everywhere with strings of tiny white lights. The roofs of hundreds of wooden stalls were decorated with seasonal scenes. No plastic imitations here, all real holly and greenery, their fragrance wafting through the throng. The little ice rink was crowded with people holding hands as they glided across, urged on by laughing friends and family. It was the final day of evening shopping before Christmas, and office workers streamed into the market for last-minute presents, hot food, beer and chats with friends, before they left for the holiday at their family homes high in the Alb. The Christmas Eve meal was always a family affair and all the shops closed at midday.

Two young girls played flutes, not for money but to entertain, their breath shooting into the cold air, their small bodies swathed in bulky coats, scarves and woollen hats. In that typically German way they played excellently, setting an ethereal background to the tenor murmur of the crowd.

At the centre of the market we came across Karl-Heinz and Rosa waiting for drinks of Glühwein, huddling near the stall for warmth. They beamed to see us, shook our hands. Before we knew it we had hot glasses in our gloved fingers and were talking in a mix of German and English about the coming holiday. Rosa sat on one of the tall stools cuddling her glass, Karl-Heinz propped up the bar, everyone smiling and happy, cheeks red and eyes bright. Darkness fell as people squeezed past each other, the smell of hot Bratwurst and sugary strawberries mixing with wine and beer and holly, the square a lively, milling place of muffled talk, bursts of laughter, and stalls laden with baskets, nick-nacks, Spätzle and Lebkuchen. People carrying large parcels edged past others holding glass mugs of hot wine; women with bulging shopping bags wove between groups of cheerful young clerks and trainees; and the air steamed with words and good wishes.

Then, with perfect timing, snow started to fall; so we stood clutching our hand-warming glasses in the cold air with snowflakes on our eyelashes and shoulders, steam rising from our drinks and mouths, hardly believing this wasn't just a fairy-tale.

It snowed heavily that winter so that, as roads were cleared, frozen mounds two metres high lined every road and lane. Everyone, it seemed, went to the ski slopes during the holiday, using their expensive equipment and enjoying the cold air and freedom; and making use of their mandatory winter car tyres.

But winter eventually started to thaw and, as spring sent out its vanguard, we too stretched out, driving west from the city through the Black Forest, the Schwarzwald, high on the road towards Baden Baden near Freudenstadt, looking for the spring.

There, we came across an area where suddenly the trees disappeared and the views widened to far distant hills. This was where in 1999 an unprecedented hurricane hit the forest with gusts of over 200 miles an hour. It flattened three million trees. An awe-inspiring place, it was a testament to the power of nature. Logging companies had removed many of the fallen trees, but the German authorities had left one area just as it was and created a trail through the devastation.

We pulled in at the layby and followed the circular trail. It wasn't a long walk but it took over an hour as we stopped to take in the enormity of tall trees being toppled one on another at huge force for mile upon mile. Nothing had been introduced along the trail. It took us over fallen tree trunks with steps cut into them, had us ducking under huge brittle roots torn violently from the earth. There was a bridge built from the dead wood to create a viewpoint, and archways sawn out of horizontal trees under which we walked on crackling dead boughs and the snow lying in the hollows. We stepped up to the top of a fallen trunk and around us was a world of almost alien and incomprehensible destruction.

But among the debris we saw new shoots already thrusting their way up among the broken boughs and scattered branches, a sign of hope and recovery. It was a small symbol but one which reminded us of nature's resilience. It was a peaceful place, one to soothe the spirit and put life into proportion. In spring the sun was warm there as we stood among the devastation with the sunlight sparkling on the remains of the winter snow.

ALPHA SEASON III.
2006-2007

Going Global...
The grant from The Arts Council had paid for the publication of *Alpha Writers* but there was still some money left for yet another big leap of our small group into the big world.

We bought a domain and set up a web site.

Sally, an experienced gardening journalist and regular writer of online columns and blogs, volunteered her technological savvy and spent months setting up the Alpha Writers' web site. She consulted the group for preferences in appearance and content and by the time Alpha Season III started we were ready to face the entire cyber-world, tell them who we were, what we did and what our interests were.

One of Sally's stories is featured below.

Zooming in...

Small scale...
Inside the group we continued the tasks we all enjoyed: challenges, sharing news of members' amazing writing exploits, and a group project which is still filed on our web site:
> *"The venture is a little different this year – but the idea is that every member will write a chapter of a book. It will be a 'Circular' book – i.e. it doesn't matter which chapter you*

start at, you just read all the chapters one after the other until you get back to where you started. The way that this will be done is that every member will create a well-defined adult character. All the characters will then be placed in a circle in a random order, and each member will write a chapter (in effect a short story) about the character he/she created, and the one on the left."

Big Scale...
David suggested writing a novella in a different genre. He set the ball rolling with a science fiction first chapter. Seven members took part in this venture, developing the novella chapter by chapter.

A Flower for Skalla was completed in November 2006. It's an excellent read and a great achievement on the part of the seven collaborators.

E-publishing was not in our competences at the time. We waited until 2010-2012 when Rosemary had acquired the necessary skills to proceed with both e-books and paperback publications. By then we had quite a collection to offer our readers.

Alpha Season III, Challenge 1 had the following brief:

'Write to convey the feeling of apprehension – a situation which may/will affect your life but waiting for it to happen seems interminable. Stop short of the happening, though. 300 words.'

Here's Zena's winning entry:
Unknowing is innocence. While I don't know I have hope. I dawdle on the way home, stoop to pick up an acorn,

wonder why there are so few cars parked here, feel my shoe rubbing. The sky is cloudy blue, the sun is warm, birds are singing, the world holds promise. I like this hope, this optimism. How can the news be bad? But farther on, the pavement's cracked, the gutter full of paper, the bushes wilting. How can it be good news? Decay is all around, the world mocks my hope. Every small mark and rough edge shouts it.

I know the test results must arrive soon, today may be the day. We'll know what illness he has, if it's the dreaded one. I breathe in deep draughts of blameless air. My legs are trembling.

Music floats from an open window, beautiful notes lifting my spirits. Or are they consoling notes, lamenting the gloom to come? A wind sifts the trees, every leaf quivering as if dancing to the tune. Beyond, the sky slides past, hugely drifting, a vast backdrop to the marionettes. Do they shiver with anticipation, or fear? Or are they blithely ignorant, moving to a rhythm of life which I'm unable to hear? They flicker and twitch, the sky glides, my feet are heavy, but soon I must arrive. Soon I will know and the leaves will be still. The gliding will cease and all will stand still as the knowing comes to me.

Whether tomorrow birds will sing through bright dancing leaves, or dusty papers blow in the gutter, only the me beyond the knowing knows.

The Alpha Decade Book Contribution vaguely inspired by the brief:

The Purple Dress
Written by Sally.
"She was all dressed in purple, you know – lovely, she

was."

There. I've done it again. Silly me. Must have said that out loud. That poor man, what's he thinking? I did like the sparkles.

"...On her dress, they were. Lovely sparkles."

"Hello," he says. He's got a nice gentle voice. Such a smart suit. Look at him, all dressed up and nowhere to go. "How are you today, then? Are you all right?"

I smile at him. He's a nice man. My Jack was a nice man. He was smart, too. I haven't seen Jack for a long time. Not since Laura went. Dear, sweet Jack.

"He was lovely, my Jack. Do you know where he's gone?"

He's coming closer. I'm not sure I like that. I back off. Keep some distance.

He stops. "Are you getting enough to eat?" he asks. I'm not sure what to do. His face is niggling at my memory. I think he might be that man who came yesterday. Nice man, he was. Probably one of those people from the hostel. They're always trying to get you to go to the hostel to stay the night, but I only tried it once. Noisy, it was. And some funny people there. You know – a bit wrong in the head.

"I'm not like that, you know. I'm not. Not like those others."

He's smiling now. A little sadly, perhaps, but a kind smile.

"No, I know you're not."

He's a kind man. Secretly, I sometimes wonder if I am. *They* think so. 'Catastrophic mental breakdown', that's what they call it. That's another reason I don't go to the hostel. They're always trying to get me to take pills. I'm too quick for them though. Don't want any of that muck.

His smile reminds me of Laura. She was kind like that.

She had a lovely smile too. She could light up a room when she smiled. She was smiling the day she went out in her pretty purple dress,

"...All sparkles. So sparkly. I liked the sparkles."

"I can get you some pizza if you like. Ham and pineapple? Your favourite, that, isn't it? Like you had yesterday? Are you hungry?"

Usually I'm hungry. Today I'm full. I found a whole cheese sandwich on top of that grit box on the corner of the Strand this morning. Not even opened. That was a feast.

"I liked the cheese. It was good cheese."

"I expect it was." That smile again. "I'll go and get it, shall I? Would you like to come with me? We can go to that place on the corner perhaps?"

I peer at him through my fringe. I'm wondering what he wants. They usually want something. Those religious types were sniffing around last week. They're good for a bowl of soup but you've got to watch them. They make you think they're being kind when really all they want is for you to join them and dress up in orange robes or go to some church or other every week.

And there was that time it got nasty, too. Those boys – they were laughing. They pushed me. Chucked my trolley in the road. Nicked my comb. I minded that. I kept my hair nice till they took my comb, and now look at it, all tangled. They were nasty. They made me cross and scared. I tried to hit them and

"...make them go away! Don't want them! Get rid of them!" But they just laughed some more...

Oh there I go again. And my eyes are leaking again too. Can't seem to stop myself these days. Are you all right, he says. I'm not all right. Not at all. I'm

"...all wrong. All wrong, all wrong, all wrong..."

"Oh no... don't worry, I'm sorry, I didn't mean to upset you." He really looks as if he might cry. Right here, in the middle of Trafalgar Square. Just like that.

I take a long look at him. I don't think he's one of the bad ones. I can spot them, these days. I keep clear. But I don't want to keep clear of this one. He's got kind eyes, and he's handsome "...just like my Jack, you know. When he was younger. He was a good-looking lad. He wore a suit, too."

We were both quite the couple when we stepped out. We would go to tea dances and everyone else would stand back and admire us as we took the floor.

"He could dance, my Jack. Can you dance? Like Jack could?"

He's smiling properly now. He holds his arms out. Well. What would you have done? A girl doesn't get an invitation like that every day.

So I drop my trolley just like that and we dance, just the two of us, under the gaze of one of those great bronze lions, and people are staring at us but I'm in a tea room in Barnstaple and I'm twenty years old again and my feet are light over the ground.

He's humming as we circle the lion, ignoring the catcalls "Oy! Mate! Find a room!" "Bet you say that to all the bag ladies!" "'Ere, can I have the next dance darlin'?" And the sniggers. They're coming over now, laughing and pointing.

I don't like it. I stop dancing. I break away and back off, grabbing my trolley and stumble a little as I speed up. Nasty men.

"...get away. Get AWAY!" I flail my carrier bag at them blindly, not caring who it hits. They're laughing. Laughing...

I fall on the ground, my trolley clattering into the road, but he's running at them now, "Leave her alone! Get lost!

Go find something else to pick on, you little toerags!" He's practically snarling, his fists clenched. They're still jeering now, but it's half-hearted. They're backing off. He's tall, he is. You wouldn't want to mess with him. So like my Jack.

He was like that with Laura's boyfriend, I remember. The one with the car. He didn't like him. Said he was feckless, that was the word he used. Hated him taking our Laura out, especially in that souped-up noisy thing he had. I told him not to interfere but turns out he was right. He waved her off, too, Jack did, that night she went off with him and never came back. They found the wreck in the morning. Instant, they said. Never would have felt a thing.

I felt, though. I felt so many things I couldn't keep them all in my head at the same time. They blew me apart, those feelings I had when they closed the door and the house went quiet. When they closed the door and shut me in. And Jack tried to help but he was in the same state as me. Worse, if anything. Our beautiful Laura. And we were both locked in that house full of terrible feelings until I could stand it no more and I had to go, I had to get out, so I went too. And I never came back, either.

The nice man turns back to me. "Are you all right?"

I pick myself up, dust down my coat, pick up my carrier bag and check inside: all still there, Laura's hair clip and Jack's old brown hat he wore all the time, all safe, nothing missing. I clutch it to me and stare around, looking for my trolley, scraping my fringe out of my eyes. I wish I had a comb. I kept my hair really nice until those boys took my comb, they were

"...nasty men. Nasty men. Make them go away. Don't want them! Get rid of them!"

"It's OK. It's OK. They're gone. It's fine. Look, here's your trolley, right here. It's not even damaged, look.

Here…"

I snatch the trolley from him fiercely. What does he want with my trolley? It's got everything I own in there. It's my trolley, he's got no right with it. He needs to leave it alone. It's my stuff. Mine. They're all the same, these do-gooders. They just want something from you all the time. You've just got to figure out what. He can't have my trolley. He can't, it's mine.

I'm backing off fast now. "Get away from me! Go away! Leave me alone!"

He's got his hands up now, standing back. "All right, I'm sorry. I'm sorry. Look, what about that pizza? What about if you just sit on that bench over there and I'll get you some? Just stay there. Right there. OK?"

I lower myself slowly onto the bench, thinking I'll just wait till he's in the queue, and then I'll get away. He'll never even know I'm gone. There, he's a long way away now. I get up and gather my things and walk off as quick as I can. Just one glimpse over my shoulder as I leave the square and I can see him.

He's just standing there, staring at me, looking so hopeless, so desolate, he makes me stop in my tracks. I'm trying to think where I've seen him before. He seems like such a nice man. Just like my Jack. My lovely Jack.

I grip my trolley firmly and turn away. Head down, I start walking away. It was lovely, her dress. All purple. She had sparkles on her dress, you know. I did like the sparkles.

ALPHA SEASON IV.
2007-2008

Composition...
As a group we'd already composed three works of fiction in unison. First *The Scribeham Chronicle,* then the as yet unnamed *Circular Book,* and now also our science fiction novella, *A Flower for Skalla.* These were intended to be read as the work of a homogeneous group using roughly the same style and theme.

In Season IV we decided to liberate the individual writer and compile an anthology on the theme of Music.

This time our contributions stood out for their wide variety of style and approach. They demonstrated the strength of our members' creative talents and we filed them until we were ready to publish them in 2011.

But that's another story.

Learning the Craft...
Olaf remained at the helm to steer a steady course, but there was no teaching involved in our group activities.

And yet we learned so much from working together, experimenting with styles and discussing writing related matters.

Each season there was a small, but healthy turnover in membership and 'newbies' soon recognised the benefits of our methods.

The annual review of Alpha which appeared in Writers' News in July 2008 testifies to this:

Reflections On A First Year With Alpha Writers
Compiled jointly by Rosemary and Tara

> *To be honest, I had no idea what to expect when I was accepted as a member of Alpha. Before the season began, I was both nervous and excited, but the other members were welcoming and friendly from the beginning.*
> *The standard of work is very high and really pushes me to raise my game. I have such respect for my colleagues' work that I anticipate the results of challenges as though they were the top prize winning competitions.*
> *My writing experience is not as extensive as many other Alpha members, and I've learned a lot from them. The topics we've discussed have been helpful and enjoyable. I feel I've made some very special friends, whom I can now approach for advice.*

We learnt from each other. School was relegated to the past; a theme one could grow nostalgic about by setting it as a challenge brief.

Alpha Season IV, Challenge 8:

'You have been offered your first commission for 'Best of Times', a nostalgia magazine. They want you to **describe your first day at school** (any time period, real or fictional). 300 words.'

Here's the winning entry, by Geoff:
Crates of warm milk stacked in the sun with the rumps of cream-snaffling sparrows twitching from the bottle-tops. Giggling girls bouncing over a skipping rope and darting across hopscotch squares. The rag-and-bone man yelling "Good luck!" as his horse and cart clattered along the lane. What exciting memories for a nipper on his first day at primary school!

I remember how noisy it seemed after our peaceful cottage by the hop fields. First, though, we had to deal with the tearful goodbyes as we lost sight of our mothers and entered the gloomy, creaky schoolroom where Mrs Nelmes towered menacingly above us. Her glare soon dissolved into a welcoming smile worthy of the "Ah! Bisto!" advert, as she launched us on the adventure of a lifetime.

1950's England was blessed with an innocence long since brutalised. On that crisp, September morning my senses were assailed by new experiences: the toilets with the rank smell of communal peeing and creosote; the musty air raid shelter next door; the radio interference as the Home Service was tuned to Music and Movement's "Row, row, row your boat..."; the clinking of satchel buckles; the immaculate rows of plimsolls; the gusto of alphabet chanting... it all seemed so wonderfully grown up.

Well, it did until Maurice Gunner dipped his finger in his inkwell and flicked black ink across Linda Cogger's pigtails. That temporary blip and ensuing hilarity prompted Mrs Nelmes to shed the smile. She strode across the heavily knotted floorboards to her gleaming wooden cupboard with its striking scent of polish. Slowly easing open the door, she extracted... Black Bess, the deadly slipper. Nobody escaped two slaps, even luckless Linda, but this punishment was never required again. We understood. We couldn't wait to get home but we were excited to come back for more.

This Alpha Decade contribution was inspired by the Season IV brief:

First Day at Big School.
Written by Suzanne.

Mum is fussing around me, straightening the navy velour hat that I'd placed at a jaunty angle and now she's untwisting the ribbon. It's hot and itchy and how I hate it already. Even more so than the green and navy striped tie which is in danger of choking me.

"Granny would have been so proud…"

I think she's going to cry so I turn away quickly. Just then I catch sight of myself in the hall mirror: navy blazer, grey tunic (length above the knee carefully measured), fawn knee-length socks and, of course, sensible brown shoes. I can still recall the argument in the shoe shop. Only yesterday I'd been tearing around the old garage site on my bike with Alan from down the road, clad in comfy trousers and T-shirt. Now I'm unrecognisable in this scratchy uniform.

I jump at the sound of the doorbell. I can see two indistinct figures through the frosted glass but I know who they are.

"Here's Julia and Maria to take you to the bus." Mum did always state the obvious.

To my horror they are laughing at me. Well, they aren't really but I sense they are fighting back girlish sniggers. Their hats are worn at jaunty angles so I push mine back again in defiance. Mum tries to give me a goodbye kiss but

I dodge out of the way and follow the two older girls out of the gate and off we set on my new adventure – my first day at "big school".

Julia is Alan's big sister – I think she's about 14 or so. I've been into her bedroom and she has grown-up things like nail varnish. Mum disapproves of her I know, but at least she's going to get me on the bus safely this morning. Maria's family originally came from Cyprus, an unbelievably exotic-sounding place for the likes of me. Devon is the furthest I've ever been out of Derbyshire. Maria announces that she has her O-level exams at the end of this school year and that she's feeling sick with nerves already. They sound like awful things to be avoided.

It's a short distance to the bus stop if we take the short cut through the jetty. Mum has told me if I'm ever on my own I must walk the long way round, as there are "naughty men" who might loiter there. She didn't enlighten me with any further details. Soon we join a chattering group of girls, similarly dressed, but no one else is wearing such a pristine uniform as mine and nobody is carrying a smart brown leather briefcase that feels heavy even though it's empty. Mum has carefully folded my PE kit into a green checked cloth bag with my name embroidered on it. I sling this over my shoulder but it keeps falling off. At last the double-decker lurches round the corner and we scramble on. I daren't risk hauling my briefcase up the stairs so I fall into the nearest seat. Julia flops down beside me.

"If a prefect gets on you have to stand and offer her your seat." I'm worried in case I don't recognise one and cause offence. I don't even know what a prefect is. The bus gathers speed along the inner ring road and I wish I could think of something to talk about to pass the time. In fact it's Julia who leans towards me.

"Do you know what a Durex is?" She stares at me intently and I believe I can even see a touch of strictly-against-the rules mascara as she blinks expectantly.

"Of course," I squeak.

Something inside tells me it wouldn't be a good idea to ask Mum that evening.

Fifteen minutes later I'm being herded into the school hall with what seems like hundreds of other nervous-looking first years and thankfully they are all dressed like me: perfect hats, straight ties and clean shoes. The hall reeks of floor polish. I take a deep breath and gaze around me. There are wooden boards boasting the names of former head girls and glass cabinets displaying silver cups. I don't think I want to be on the list of head girls but I long to hold one of those shiny trophies. I'm not yet sure for what achievement. Maybe netball captain? I join the correct line when my name is called and we're marched off to our form room on the first floor. I'm terrified that I'll get lost so I concentrate hard, try to look for landmarks to remember but most importantly I note where the toilets are. It's obvious where the staff room is as a pungent fug of smoke seeps out even when the door is closed.

Miss Mann, our form teacher, is large and fierce. She wears a long black gown, no stockings and open-toed sandals. She barks out our names in alphabetical order then says we have to learn the order so we can shout our names for the morning register. To my disgust there are five other girls in my form also called Susan and I curse my parents' choice. Unlike most of my classmates I don't even have a middle name so I'm tempted to invent one. I think I'll be Susan Joanna.

I arrange my new exercise books in my desk and make a mental note to bring a photo of David Cassidy to pin onto the inside lid – or maybe a picture of the Derby County football team? No, I decide that to fit in with the other girls, a pop star would be a better choice. Caroline chats to me at break. I'm relieved to see at least one face from my primary school. Most of my old friends have gone to another secondary school because of the strict catchment area rules. I think Caroline's from a posh district though, as her Mum drives a Volvo.

"Daddy wants me to do well and become a barrister," Caroline tells me as we stand at the edge of the school field. I'd no idea what a barrister did but that seemed a safer question to ask Mum tonight.

After break it's history. Miss Williams announces that we're going to study Egypt this term. I wonder if it's near Cyprus. I might ask Maria on the bus later on. Miss Williams is dressed like so many of the other teachers I've already spotted: tweedy type of skirt, cardigan and flat shoes. (Only Miss Mann wears a gown.) E G Y P T... E G Y P T... Miss Williams chants as she marches around the rows of desks, looking carefully at what we have written on the first page of our exercise books. She spits out the letters one by one and a little blob smudges my beautifully written title. My work is scruffy already but at least I can spell Egypt.

Our French teacher is a breath of fresh air. She's young and lively, with bobbed brown hair and wears large, dark-framed glasses. She smiles encouragingly as we try to repeat: *le ciel est bleu, le soleil brille* in our Derby accents. I decide that French is my favourite subject and I can't wait to take my textbook home to cover in sticky-backed plastic.

The rest of the day passes in a blur. The science lab is scary, gym in navy knickers embarrassing, but not so much so as the compulsory shower afterwards. We sidle through in a timid line, our arms crossed to hide little breasts in various stages of development as Miss Rowlands supervises. She's comfortably concealed in her navy tracksuit, a whistle dangling around her neck at the ready to challenge any disobedience.

At the 4 o'clock bell we stand silently behind our chairs and wait to be dismissed. There's a line of buses at the gate and I panic until I find the right one. I see Julia and Maria but they ignore me – after all they've done their babysitting duty for today. I grab a seat then I spot a tall slender girl with glossy dark hair that spills out from beneath her hat. She is wearing tan coloured tights, not socks, and a prefect badge on her blazer lapel. She's holding on to the handrail, balancing briefcase and cookery basket, yet she still looks serene. I can't believe I'll ever look so grown-up. I suddenly remember Julia's advice.

"Would you like to sit down?" My words come out shyly.

"Oh, thank you. That's really kind." She smiles at me and I'm in love..

ALPHA SEASON V.
2008-2009

Main Characters...
Olaf's original idea of running an email writers' group for one year as an experiment had long ago burst out of its boundaries. Our group had become a firm fixture with a settled routine and a dedicated membership with no intention of quitting.

Olaf had heroically shouldered the burden of organising a stimulating programme year in, year out. A number of tasks had found volunteers and Olaf was beginning to enjoy being an active member rather more than being the leader.

When Season V started Olaf appointed David as his Steward. David had been assisting Olaf for a while and he was ready to take over his duties with the full support of members (and still closely monitored by Olaf).

Inspiration...
David soon had the group dancing to his tune. One of the first ventures he launched was another group writing project. He often joked about the many unfinished novels he had stashed away under his bed and from this store he chose the opening chapter of a crime novel and asked for volunteers to complete it. To add a special touch he asked for every chapter to begin and end with a phone call.

Say n' more
This took shape over the season and the final novella was 22,500 words long. A complex intrigue with wide-reaching repercussions gradually jelled into a riveting story full of suspense. It flows smoothly as if written by one author: The Alpha Writer.

Our usual routine of challenges continued with all members exploring how to write on a variety of themes. One of our challenges had the following brief:

Alpha Season V, Challenge 7:

'Write a story conveying the feeling of **Terror** in 300 words.'

The following entry, written by Sue, was one of the winners:
I can't stay here but it feels like the safest place. Tucked in my corner, safe, quiet, but if I move I will be heard. Paralysed with fear from no stimulus – no noise, no smoke, just deathly quiet. Outside the window no traffic moves, no birds sing, nothing – the city is quiet. Waiting. Crouched, stiff, I feel myself needing to shift. Slowly from my safe corner I unfold my aching body. I stretch my body, legs getting pins and needles. My spine cracks as it straightens, my eyes shifting in the gloom. My ears are straining, listening for something, anything. Sharp in the dark. There, what was that? Just a disturbance in the air. It's coming. My body gets ready to go. I can hear my breath rasping through my nose, my chest heaving from the effort of my respiration. I can feel my heart pounding in my chest as if it's trying to escape my body. The roar of the blood in my ears as it races around my body.

Shaking from the effort of being still I begin to move.

Adrenaline coursing now through my body as the time has come to flee. I grope through the dark, I have to get into the light now, outside in the air, from this dark building. Panting with fear I am disoriented my body is covered in sweat. My head turns frantically – which way? Panic is trying to set in, I must fight it. There, a light, is it the right way? Here goes.

This Alpha Decade contribution was inspired by the Season V brief:

A Cold Day In Hell.
Written by Chris.

"...sick and disabled claimants will be assessed to judge their capability for work..."

It was a cold day in hell. Snowflakes mingled with falling ash but in the eerie light it was hard to tell one from the other. The new arrivals staggered from the train, some shivering, others looking around with a desperate defiance, most clinging to each other's bodies and humanity, too numb to take in their surroundings.

Hannah stamped her feet on the gritty soil. She felt even more dirty than tired, and she was utterly exhausted after the endless, cramped, unlit, unventilated, unfed, unwatered hours on the train; she longed for a bathroom, some running warm water, clean towels. Cloaked by a dull despair she stared at a large set of iron gates close by, and which seemed to be surmounted by some metal work motto. She squinted.

"It's German," a voice said, to her left.

She jumped and gasped.

A young man, tall, good-looking, smiled shyly. "Sorry, I didn't mean to startle you."

Hannah noticed a gold tooth in his smile and tried to respond, but no words came.

"I'm Simon. Do you know any German?"

Hannah shook her head, as more people fell off the train and banged into her from behind. She heard cursing. And behind it, the sound she had been hearing constantly for the past three days: an old woman weeping.

"Let's move out of the way." Simon steered her a few yards away from the train. "Are you with anyone?"

Hannah shook her head again. In the distance she saw a group of uniformed, armed men marching towards them.

"Stay near me," Simon muttered, and in his tone she heard an uncertain mix of question and command.

Hannah watched the arrival of the man whose face wasn't there. The only officer, at the head of a small squad, he stood out amongst the drab panic all around with his leather trench coat and peaked cap. She saw a flat, broad, rather ordinary face, with high cheekbones and eyes set a little too far apart. But it was not his appearance that compelled her attention, it was something else. Despite her misery and discomfort, she couldn't drag her eyes away from him. He was staring at the terrified rabble in front of him, and though Hannah tried, from her vantage point behind Simon's back, she failed to recognise any expression that might have been expected from him: no anger, no contempt, no humour, no fanaticism, no cruelty. She saw eyes. Eyes that calmly looked around and seemingly took in everything, but she could not see the tell-tale spark that was the ordinary, unremarked sign of consciousness. Eyes that did not betray for a moment that they were seeing other human beings. (When she used to go to the cinema, she would play a game with herself - if there was a close-up of an actor on screen, speaking, she would decide whether or not he or she was looking another person in the eye. She could always tell; eyes register when they meet the eyes of someone else.)

It was the same here. Eyes in a face. But eyes and a face without anything behind them. And therefore a face that might as well not be there. Was NOT there in any sense of the word she understood. His body was there, yes it was commandingly and compellingly there; Hannah noticed several people watching him, and she even saw more than one woman, her normal instincts pulling her for one brief moment out of her present misery, pat her hair before the banging chaos reaffirmed the present nightmare. His soul? How did you see a soul, how did you mark its presence? She was no philosopher. She could not answer this question, but yet she intuitively knew that the thing she took for granted in every human being, in the meanest wretch who had arrived on the train, in the small squad of soldiers standing alertly to one side… was not visible in this man.

"…company who won the contract for assessments, will earn bonuses based upon how many claimants are judged fit for work. These claimants will be transferred to unemployment benefits…"

Hannah shook her head to clear it, and at that moment was startled to feel a rifle butt hit her in the back. She jumped forward and turned to see an armed guard about to strike her again.

"Move!" he shouted in German.

"Move!" another guard shouted, in Dutch.

She stumbled forward, and looked for Simon. He was

bending over just a short distance away, attending to what she first thought was a bundle of rags on the ground. Then she realised that the sound of weeping - that very particular rasping, constant, wheezing anguish she had endured hearing all throughout the journey - had stopped. With the chaos all around, the shouts, barked orders, cries and the slamming of cattle-truck doors, she had stopped registering it, but now she was aware that one sound had been replaced by a tiny island of silence amid the hubbub.

Simon was struck by a rifle butt on the side of the head just as she saw him do something among the rags. He fell sideways and was hauled up by a guard who struck him again in the back and urged him forward.

Hannah stumbled towards him and the two kept company as the pathetic line was bullied towards the gates. "Was she…?" whispered Hannah.

Simon nodded grimly. "Yes. I just managed to close her eyes and say a brief prayer, before…" He fell silent.

The train journey had been a filter, one that stripped the suave, the sophisticated, and the civilised from the rat-trapped travellers. The end result was raggedness that seeped everywhere, like a stain: the straggling line that was driven like cattle through the waiting gates, the group of ragged musicians standing just inside who played a ragged march, the ragged sky that poured its grey down on everything - everything in fact, except the casual, unstudied, uniformed superiority of the man whose face wasn't there.

As they passed beneath the gates, they both looked up. "German," muttered Simon." "'Work makes you free'."

Hannah shuddered.

"…claimants will be placed into one of two groups - those

declared to be fit for work, and those found to have limited or no capability for work..."

It was cold on the ramp. Miraculously, Simon and Hannah managed to avoid being separated and now stood listening to the instructions being issued dispassionately by The Man Whose Face Wasn't There, and translated into Dutch by a squad member wearing a striped blue and white uniform. These, they later learned, were fellow-prisoners, which raised more uncomfortable questions: why were there prisoners doing the Germans' work for them? Were they also Dutch Jews? What had they gained from this 'special work'?

Hannah tried to concentrate on the Dutch translation.

"... a medical inspection by our doctor. If assessed and found suitable to work right away, you will go and stand in a line to the right. Otherwise we will assign you to other duties and you will go and join the line to the left. Please make yourselves ready for the inspection." A small man wearing an officer's uniform and round, metal-framed spectacles stepped forward and began walking along the line. He would pause before each prisoner, look them up and down for a second or two, and then issue a curt two-word instruction: *"nach rechts"* (to the right) or *"nach links"* (to the left).

Hannah began to notice that most men of working age were assigned to the right, while children, the elderly, the obviously unwell or disabled, and many women, were directed to the left.

The crush in front thinned and vanished and the doctor was now surveying Simon. *"Nach rechts."*

Simon began to walk towards the lengthening line and the doctor, half watching him, and half attending to his job, barely bothered to look at Hannah. *"Nach links."*

Hannah saw Simon pause and stop. He looked over his shoulder and cried out, "No!"

The doctor turned back in obvious disbelief, summoned the translator with a gesture and muttered at him briefly, pointing to Simon. The translator went over and spat in Simon's face. "You dare to question the authority of the officer, you vermin?"

Simon wiped his face and Hannah could see him jerk forward slightly, then restrain himself. The translator started screaming at him in Dutch, telling him he would learn respect, would soon enough realise where he was, would be shot in an instant if he didn't move immediately to where he'd been told to go.

During all this, the Man Whose Face Wasn't There had been talking to a couple of fellow officers who had arrived to supervise the two lines. Hearing the commotion, he walked towards the doctor and asked him something quietly in German. The doctor replied swiftly, spreading his hands in a gesture that clearly indicated that the matter was all under control. The officer nodded, and made to rejoin his former conversation. Then, on what seemed to be a whim, he walked over to Simon and indicated that he should rejoin the crowd on the ramp. Simon went and stood next to Hannah, and the translator was summoned.

"Is this your wife?"

Simon shook his head. "No sir."

"Your sister, your girlfriend?"

Simon again shook his head. "Someone I met when we arrived here. I just thought that she would make a good worker, sir. She is young and fit." The officer stared at Simon for a good minute, and Simon stared back without blinking.

Then it was Hannah's turn to be surveyed, though

curiously it was not the top-to-bottom-and-back of the doctor's 'assessment'; he simply allowed his eyes to circle all around her face and finally directly into her eyes.

Hannah had once again the eerie sense of a void behind the man's face, that she might be looking at… not a machine exactly, nor the embodiment of evil, but something where a dimension was distinctly missing. Close up, this sensation was exactly the same as her earlier impression.

Finally, the man nodded, as if he had made a decision. He looked at Simon. *"Nach rechts"* and pointed with his head. Simon walked towards the right-hand line without looking back. The officer looked at Hannah for another long moment, and then repeated *"nach rechts"*. Again he pointed to the line and Hannah knew there was no expectation of thanks or of any other expression of emotion.

She swallowed and followed Simon towards the waiting line. Neither of them saw the man and the doctor salute each other and click their heels. The doctor resumed his slow walk along the crowd on the ramp, the man rejoined the other officers. A fly had buzzed and been swatted. The incident was over.

Hannah didn't have time to mourn her hair or learn to accept her cold, bare, itching scalp. Her skin was burning after being doused in pesticide, her blue stripey uniform was too big and her shoes were too small. Yet even these discomforts were somehow swallowed up in a nightmarish 'tour' of a cramped, spartan, unheated, almost unlit barrack. She sat on a bunk and tried to think of Simon. He had become a symbol for her of the vanished world she remembered, a world of warmth, of fashions, of culture, of love. She had known him for less than an hour, and yet he lived inside her as her one single friend in this sea of human misery.

There had been a woman, another prisoner. She had explained to Hannah what her new life was to be. Now she returned. Earlier she had been brusque but not harsh. Now she grabbed Hannah and pulled her up from the bunk. Her fingers hurt and Hannah cried out then bit her lip, ashamed.

"You've no time for this," the woman hissed. "There will be not one second of your life that is not accounted from now on." She relaxed her grip a little and drew Hannah slowly to the nearest grimy window. She pointed to the left. "Look," was all she said.

Hannah looked. She saw other bleak barracks like the one they stood in, and saw a few hunched prisoners shuffling their stripes from one unknown web to another. In the distance a very tall brick chimney vomited a column of black smoke that bent sideways and sank slowly towards the camp, covering everything with a film of ash.

"See that?" said the woman. "That chimney? That's the crematorium." She looked away as if she were not sure whether to say any more, then turned quickly back to face Hannah. "That line to the left on the ramp, the one you nearly ended up in?"

Hannah nodded.

The woman sighed and drew Hannah back from the window. "That's them."

Hannah stared, not comprehending. Then slowly, with a horrible dawning, an understanding settled on her like the film of ash over the camp. Suddenly she grasped just exactly where she was, what the whole ghastly scheme was about. Her legs gave way, her head spun…

…and she awoke with a gasp, sweating and disoriented. She lay back for several minutes to recover her sense of 'where' and 'when', then shook her head to clear it. She began the long process of transferring from bed to wheelchair. Half an hour later she wheeled in to join her family at breakfast.

"Mum, do we have any Dutch ancestors?"

"Not as far back as I know, love. But that's not very far. Why do you ask?"

"Oh, nothing really. It was just something I..." She shook her head. "It's not important."

Her mother smiled, turned away and switched on the grill. Hannah shuddered. Her father looked up from his newspaper. "Is it your assessment today, Hannah?" She nodded.

"Good luck." He pointed to the front page headline in his tabloid. Hannah made out the word SCROUNGERS. "You won't have anything to worry about, not like these workshy layabouts they're trying to flush out."

Hannah helped herself to toast. "*Arbeit macht frei,*" she muttered under her breath.

ALPHA SEASON VI.
2009-2010

Esoteric...
Writers often stumble across puzzling points that only other writers would be interested in. Alpha Writers get considerable pleasure out of discussing these. When somebody asked where on earth the word 'gallimaufry' had come from we dived into a discussion that teetered between the humorous and the learned. Later we had our own very enjoyable challenge to create new words.

Another lively debate ensued when a member condemned the use of 'posh' words. We should avoid all Latin-based words like the pest. The impossibility of such a rule surprised many.

'Screamers' were also reviled. No writers worth their salt need exclamation marks or bold lettering.

Dashes and ellipses ... there are many different points of view and we can get quite carried away in these debates.

Ramifications...
The novellas proved our combined skills. The challenges brought out members' ambition to excel individually and at the end of each season an Alpha Laureate is nominated. Clare, whose challenge entry is featured below, was Alpha Laureate for Season VI.

The Log showed how the creative surge of energy spilled into our 'real' writing world outside Alpha.

Christine (whose story is featured below) had been Log Editor since Season III. Towards the end of Season VI she wrote an article entitled *A Writers' Log – Alpha Style* which was published in *Link*, The Journal of the National Association of Writers' Groups.

Here's an extract:

> *In real life the seventeen of us practise our writing skills in roughly as many different ways. There are career writers, freelances and regular column writers in our midst with specialist subjects as diverse as horticullure, history, dogs, genealogy, statistics, botany and education. We have a handful of (not yet published) novelists, and we have (published) poets, short story writers and dramatists. We even have ghost writers, web writers and several bloggers to our credit. Some write book reviews and letters to the editor, others give talks and after-dinner speeches (...)*
>
> *Success comes in many guises. A compliment by a stranger in the street. A bunch of flowers from a happy client. An unexpected commission. An all-inclusive trip to the Caribbean to write an article. The handshake of an impressed mayor. An encouraging note added to the rejection slip. A phone call from a celebrity. Getting published. (...)*
>
> *There's no such word as failure. A finished piece of work sent out into the big, wide world is a triumph. A completed novel is a great triumph. We express our disappointments and the agony of waiting in The Log. "Still no reaction from...", "Not a word from... Ah, me!" "Didn't get anywhere in..." "What am I doing wrong?"*

One of the ten challenges of the season had the following

brief:

Alpha Season VI, Challenge 8:

'**Describe a place which is very special to you.** Give it the title "My Place". I would like to see, smell, maybe even recognize it. It could be your town, your home, your room, your chair, your office and so on, but it will have special significance for respondents. 300 words.'

This is Clare's winning entry:
I inhale as I step across the threshold – traces of incense, ozone, and clean linen – a heady mix. Amber pads in beside me and settles with a contented sigh onto her blanket in the corner.

I reacquaint myself with my surroundings – white painted floorboards, simple square wooden table and two blue director chairs, walls adorned with paintings, poetry, collages and shell pictures, a small cupboard for crockery, and of course, my little stove and kettle.

Running my fingers across the rough surface of the whitewood table, I carefully lay down my notebook and pen.

Flinging open the shutters, I drag a chair to the open door, take a deep breath, and sit. Just sit. And stare. Take in the amazing view. The waves are rolling in today, and the sound of the current pulling back on the shingle vibrates through my being. The mournful cry of the seagulls overhead, as they circle, looking hopefully for a brave tourist carrying any sort of food, reminds me it is lunchtime.

But I am not hungry. Not for food anyway. I just want to lap up this atmosphere. It is never busy here even in the height of summer, but at this time of year, Amber and I have the whole area to ourselves, apart from the gulls.

The wind is quite strong off the coast, and the white horses leap and froth. The winter sun tries gamely to spread a little warmth across the wooden balcony, casting shadow patterns on the cream and blue shutters.

The grassy slopes stretch from the quiet road above, down to the promenade below. The peace and inspiration I find here is worth far more than that I could find in expensive spas, retreat centres or hotels.

My beach hut is My Place.

This Alpha Decade contribution was inspired by the Season VI brief:

Spring Symphony
Written by Christine.

Something is tugging at the Brimstone Yellow butterfly's wings, making them twitch. His sleep has been light over the last month and he's awoken several times and fluttered around to check on the forest. He's sucked nectar from primroses and gorse. He's gone back to sleep. This time the tug is more urgent. The sun is stirring nature into action.

He feels quite dizzy as he responds to the vigour around him. Even his hibernation host, the winter-proud holly, joins in the wood chorus of life-asserting joy and shoots little spurts of sap into its branches. The modest white flowers of the holly with their heady scent are in the making, promising renewal of the bright red berries.

He hears the movements under the thick layer of last year's leaves. Warmth and nutrition are spread around, and underground, dormant systems of growth are preparing to clothe

the forest in its springtime splendour.

The butterfly cannot stay still. This time he will not content himself with a quick visit to primroses and celandines. There are far greater powers stirring inside him than mere hunger. He wants company. He wants to procreate. He knows she's looking for him out there.

Sarah straightened up from her crouching position and brushed leaves and earth off her jeans. She was pleased with the results; very pleased.

She'd done the daffodils and the anemones now, the latter just nearing their peak and standing proud – white on emerald green – at her feet. She'd check the primroses and have a quick look to see if bluebells showed signs of buds.

She picked up her equipment and packed it neatly into the case: camera, thermometer, light meter, portable microscope, knife, scissors and ruler. The notebook went in last and she checked the main details. Date: 20/03/2014. Time: 12.15pm. No. of photos: 16 so far. Temperature on the anemone patch: 7°C. Light reading: 4,380 ft-c; pretty good for the time of year.

She headed off for the primroses. The spot was carefully marked on her plan of the forest with crossing lines between four big trees; easily identifiable landmarks that led to her chosen clump.

It was near the clearing by the river favoured by picnickers, a resting place for horse riders and ideal for primary school teachers taking their classes out. Sarah suddenly remembered the white witch and wondered if she'd be there. She wasn't really a witch, of course, and she wasn't white either, but Sarah had seen her there on some of her spring outings to inspect the plants, and in her mind she called her the white witch.

The most intriguing part of it was that she was almost sure the white witch was her daughter's history teacher. She hadn't been quite close enough to her on the parents' evening, or in the woods, but...

Sarah intended to complete ten spring surveys before publishing her findings – including Granny's perceptive notes. This was her sixth year. She'd started in 2009 after Granny's death in December.

Granny had taught her how to identify plants using the Linnaean system. When Sarah was eleven her parents had been stationed overseas, and she'd stayed behind with Granny to take up her place at the grammar school rather than disrupt her education at that crucial stage.

Sarah smiled when she thought of her triumphant excitement as she sat in Granny's garden with the botany book and a daisy. She worked laboriously through all the characteristics of the plant, moving from section to section and answering the questions – like in a treasure hunt – before finally reaching the page that identified her plant: "It's a daisy!" she shouted, basking in Granny's praise for mastering the complicated process.

Granny had shown her the herbarium she'd made when she was a child. Sarah thought it was more like a scrap book with scribbled notes and pressed flowers stuck in with sticky tape. Granny had put a lot of work into it over two whole years: 1933 and 1934.

Finding the herbarium amongst Granny's belongings after her death had brought back memories. That was the first thing. But Sarah also had an idea that the information would be of great interest to those studying the effects of climate change; especially if backed up by similar notes from the present. She chose the pressed anemone and

Granny's entry for it as her starting point:

"Wood anemone: Anemone nemorosa. Found in Harewood, 21st of March 1934. Sunny, but cold."

Eighty years later Sarah was about to add her own pressed specimen, also picked on the day of the spring equinox.

Granny had added another note: "Half a mile away, on the eastern side of Harewood, the daffodils are in full bloom, 'Fluttering and dancing in the breeze'."

Sarah made a note of the entry on her own daffodil page. As for Wordsworth, she thought, let's leave him out of this.

The Brimstone Yellow butterfly chooses a sunray and travels up high along its path. He catches thermals and lulls, rising, descending and whirling in the bright, warm light. Weightless as a feather or folded tight as a bullet he's as free as the breeze: a dancing flash of yellow, bathing in the breath of the forest as it stretches upwards, engaged in the silent, slow-motion display of vegetative fireworks that is spring.

The butterfly is jubilant. This is the most exciting day of his life. He knows he'll soon find her and they'll dance in the sunlight together.

In the clearing Rachel stretched her hands up in the air as far as they'd go. Her small, agile body rose into the movement. Her four companions joined in the upward surge, their hands forming a sky-pointing cluster. Very slowly they all leaned back away from the centre, turning on the spot, their arms and bodies describing wide arcs and bending down towards the earth. They continued the circular motion, spreading their arms wide, sliding their feet softly over the ground, turning their hands palms up, palms down, before letting them glide gently towards their hearts.

They stood there silently, their spirits receptive to the forest and its equinox energy charge. Their bodies relaxed and they continued the gentle dance moves, opening up every fibre to the health-giving balance of nature; reaching, gathering, embracing.

Rachel felt tensions dissolving. In their place came peace and a spreading sense of warm joy that rolled over her like a wave. She merged into the mystery of the equinox; understood it with a part of her that wasn't her brain.

The butterfly rides on the sunbeam through the forest. He's heading purposefully towards the point where their two paths will converge: his and hers. His flight is fluid and deliberately haphazard in its singular search for life-fulfilling pleasure.

He sees the fluttering, yellow point in the distance. He sees movements that mimic his own. His flight falters; so does hers. They feel incomplete, lacking something caused by the space between them. Their wings propel them forward with unwonted speed, the separation is unbearable. They meet.

They commence the glorious dance of the rites of spring.

Sarah walked on. Primroses had a longer flowering season than anemones and daffodils which made them less significant for her survey. They could start in early February in sheltered, sunny spots. She'd checked this particular clump weekly since the beginning of March when it had been packed full of buds with several open flowers. Now it was a mass of pale, yellow blooms with new buds opening faster than older ones wilted. She took a photo and measured the size of the clump.

The bluebells wouldn't be out for another couple of

weeks. But the plants could be examined if you knew where to look for the strappy leaves. Sarah checked her map. She emerged from the hollow path and turned south. The stream was on her left and the steep slope with the bluebells on her right.

On the other side of the stream was the popular clearing where only a few slender beech trees gave shade in the summer. The ground was even and covered with last year's coppery leaves. A group of five people wearing jeans or dark tracksuits were absorbed in a series of movements; very slow and ceremonial, Sarah thought, like figures in a dance. The white witch was there, and with her, she presumed, her sorceress's apprentices.

She watched the group performing their routines. There wasn't a leader as such, yet they moved in identical patterns. Sarah felt something tugging at her own arms and legs; an urge to copy their ritual.

'That would be some joke,' she thought. 'Me casting magic spells!'

On an impulse she got her phone out and zoomed in to get a photo of the white witch. Then she wrote a text to her daughter: "Is this your bewitching history teacher?"

The two Brimstone Yellow butterflies dip and soar together. What one initiates, the other completes. They wind through spirals, they flick and flip, brush wings and shudder with joy. They're blissfully tipsy with the heady spring air. They want to dance forever. The unknown climax beyond the dance will wait till they've had their fill.

They follow the sun through the forest, weaving poetry along their passage.

When Rachel saw the yellow butterflies coming towards

them, trailing the glory of spring, she stopped in awe. With her companions she accepted their blessing. They stood in perfect stillness and watched the butterflies performing the dance of love; their love of spring, their love.

Sarah observed the hiatus and wondered what caused it. She moved forward a bit and tried to focus on some yellow dots above the group. As she glanced upward she caught the full glare of the equinoctial sun in her eyes. She blinked and shook her head. Her fumbling hands faltered and she accidentally pressed 'delete' instead of 'send'.

Thus an alternative scenario vanished from that perfect day's agenda. It's called 'the inverted butterfly effect': Sarah's daughter did not receive a photo of her teacher with a text that mentioned the 'witch' word. Sarah's daughter did not post the photo on her Facebook page and she did not forward it to all her friends at school, who subsequently did not conspire to harass and ridicule their teacher and publish the photo with insinuating comments for all and sundry to see.

The dancing butterflies continue through the forest. They flitter past the small group of people and hang for a moment above the clear waters of the stream, vibrating with its bubbling spring joy and reflecting their butterfly happiness in the watery mirror.

They hover and perform some joyous flips and flutters near the solitary figure on the other side of the stream.

Sarah saw the butterflies: spiralling, swooping, gyrating from the stream towards her. Their aerial ballet looked full of meaning, as if the butterflies had a tale to tell: a tale half glimpsed in the depths of her memory store; a tale on the point of emerging.

Granny once told her that she was brilliant at observing,

but hopeless at looking and admiring. The butterflies just reminded her of that. She watched their courtship dance as they flitted on. And, yes, she admired it, but there was more to it than that: it awed her.

She crossed the stream on the narrow wooden bridge absorbed in trying to tease out the tale at the edge of her thoughts. She wasn't thinking about the white witch and her companions and stopped abruptly when she had to pass close to them to rejoin her path.

She couldn't help it. She had to watch, just a little. Again she felt the tugging at her limbs, the strange desire to copy the slow ritual movements they performed.

Rachel and her companions noticed the spectator. They turned towards her and smiled. Then they reached out their hands in invitation, waving Sarah towards them. Hesitantly Sarah approached, drawn by their friendly gesture.

The group reiterated their basic routines, slowly to encourage Sarah to join in. They varied their gestures so naturally that Sarah soon lost her awkwardness. She no longer thought of her movements, she loosened up, she let herself go. She became part of the forest, the equinox and the group's celebration of spring. It was like a turning point when time stood still.

Eventually they paused. They looked around at the forest. Rachel took Sarah's hand and led her to one of the tall beech trees.

"Feel it!" she said. They embraced the tree, holding hands round its smooth trunk.

At first Sarah felt nothing. Then her inner eye saw the butterflies and she sensed warmth surging up through the tree. The tree's pulse was beating as the sap rose and moisture welled up in Sarah's eyes as the indomitable reassertion of life revealed itself. She squeezed Rachel's hand and Rachel returned the pressure.

They left the forest together. Rachel was delighted to learn that Sarah was Debbie's mother. Sarah wanted to know more about Qigong and whether she could join the class.

At home Sarah organised her notes. Six years' worth of methodically accumulated data was spread out in front of her on the desk. Right up until today Sarah had been very satisfied with her project, and Granny's notes would add an excellent, wider perspective.

But now there was the subject of the Brimstone Yellow butterflies. She had seen them with her own eyes

Beside the stream,
Beneath the trees,
A pair of golden butterflies,
Fluttering and dancing in the breeze

and she knew she'd missed an essential point.

In fact, today she'd outdone Wordsworth. He had merely "gazed, and gazed" while she had joined in the dance of daffodils and butterflies. And the dance had sprinkled a sparkling layer of poetry over everything.

Granny had been right: Observing was to admiring as a diagram of the birth canal was to the cry of a new-born baby.

The butterflies journey leisurely on. They weave delicate patterns around flowers and buds. They pirouette above the heaving activity of the sun-drenched loam and soar to share their delight with the sap-delirious treetops. Their happiness is boundless and their wings clap together as they whirl and twirl till their closeness reaches its climax. Clasped in a tender embrace they land in a clump of primroses where they fulfil their love and perpetuate the glory of Brimstone Yellow butterflies.

ALPHA SEASON VII.
2010-2011

Adversity...
When David found out that what he thought had been a bout of food poisoning was in fact bowel cancer, he informed Olaf and Christine. He wanted to continue writing and encouraging Alphas to write in his capacity as Alpha Steward.

Whenever David's treatment kept him away from Alpha he asked Christine to stand in for him. But it was his driving force that kept Alpha going for the whole of that season.

David died in March 2011.

Repercussions...
After the initial shock and grief the group rallied to honour David's memory. Rosemary was able to go to the funeral and she gave David's daughter a letter of condolence from all of us.

John suggested writing an anthology dedicated to David's memory, and after some discussion we agreed to write on the theme of 'Birth'.

Ten Alphas contributed to the 'Birth' anthology with four poems and six prose pieces.

Spin-off...
David's enthusiasm had spurred the group on to

collaborate in the writing of two novellas, one anthology and now – indirectly – another anthology… a considerable collection of work which group members were rather proud of.

E-publishing was becoming a factor to be reckoned with and we were in the fortunate situation to have a member who'd acquired the necessary skills to take advantage of this. Rosemary volunteered her know-how, and in June 2011 *Say n'more*, the Alpha novella which David had launched and supervised, was e-published. It was a huge feather in the cap for the Alpha Group and at the same time it was a tribute to David and we agreed that all profits should be donated to Macmillan Cancer Support.

Season VII, Challenge 4:

Most seasons we run a challenge inspired by a photo.

The photo challenge for Season VII showed a **Tudor House** and entries could be in any genre. There were poems, stories and even a non-fiction piece about architecture.

The winning entry, written by Sally:
She first saw the house on that holiday in Suffolk when it snowed on Southwold beach in June. She'd loved it straight away, viscerally, with all her heart. They'd come into the café for a cuppa, Barry moaning about the cold and the service. Opposite was a confection of black and white, ornate as a tapestry, the house she'd always dreamed of. He laughed when she told him. A lifetime of trouble: and anyway, our wardrobes would never fit those walls. Last year, it was for sale. She got the details. Fifty grand extra and they could swap it for their poky ex-council house in

the posh end of Chingford, easy commute and straight corners - they knew how to build houses then. It would be nice, she began wondering out loud, to get out of the smog, and the traffic. The neighbours were noisy... and they needed more space. He'd smiled indulgently. A phase: probably hormones, his thoughts twinkled behind his eyes. When a board appeared outside their gate the first tiny flame of panic flickered. Then the letter arrived from the Suffolk estate agents. But all our friends are here! And what about my work? We've only just paid off the mortgage... And on, and on. Well: she thought. They'd led their lives to his tune for twenty years. Now it was her turn. He could have walked, of course. He knew she couldn't afford the house without him. But she took care of that too. And here she was, walking in through the black-stained door, caressing the grooves of century-worn oak. Home, at last. He had come with her, of course, in the end. The removal men were bringing him in now, grumbling about the weight. She'd unpack the spade later. Now, where was the kettle?

This Alpha Decade contribution was inspired by the Season VII brief:

The Crossing
Written by Morgen

'If you would all like to make your way up to the Abbey, we'll have some tea before the main tour.'

Miss Kennedy, Chief Guide for the Haunted Heritage Tour Company reached up onto tiptoes, stretching her snug powder-blue uniform even tighter across her hips. She extended one perfectly manicured finger out over the heads of her charges while she counted.

'...eighteen, nineteen...where's Mr Cohen?'

Ruth Cohen looked over her shoulder. A pink baseball cap could be seen hovering above an azalea bush.

'For Chrissakes Harry. They have indoor plumbing here. We're not in Kansas.'

Harry Cohen emerged from behind the bush. His wife took his arm and they ran to catch up with the group as it followed obediently behind Miss Kennedy.

Although she couldn't see the brightly coloured gaggle as it fussed up the broad sweep toward the magnificent face of Saxonby Abbey, Morag glanced at the house, as if watching them go.

Sometimes it seemed as if she'd spent an eternity at the lakeside watching changes come upon the house. As the sun dapples a wooded walk, so it seemed to be constantly changing. Sometimes bright and hopeful with the sun gilding the roof; smiling, coaxing. Sometimes dark and vengeful, its deep hooded windows like black eyes, daring her to approach. Morag felt lost sometimes, drifting. But not today. She looked at the canopy of trees lining the drive, heavy with blossom and a little pride grew in her chest. Her father, as Head Gardener to the Hilchester family, was responsible for all the planting.

He was neither an educated man nor articulate and knew nothing of the Latin names for plants but he could create colour and heavenly scented havens where there had just been barren earth.

As a child she had loved to watch his great hands tenderly coaxing the most delicate of blooms. A giant of a man, he was as gentle as a lamb. She remembered how he'd run to rescue a butterfly being tortured by a kitten. How he'd cradled it and laid it on the grass in the shade of a camellia. He'd sat and watched it until it flew away into the sun. She'd cried and cried, but she was crying for her father, knowing his heart would break if the creature died.

Morag was at peace at the side of the lake. It was her special place. Some days the water was a dull, deep blue, still and restful as if sleeping. At other times it was black and brooding, seeming to draw at anything it sensed on the shore.

Today, though, there was no hint of menace. From her cool retreat beneath the willows, she watched as the water shimmered silver beneath the hazy sun. The surface danced as a light breeze played among the ripples.

A little tingle of excitement began to spread up from her toes, running though her body making her clutch at her dress. She closed her eyes and smiled, allowing herself to drown in the warmth of promises.

'Gee, honey. Get a load of this.'

Ruth Cohen ran her hands over the oak bed.

'It's one of those four-posted things. Wouldn't it look just swell out by the pool? Ah, c'mon Harry...the Schwarzkopfs would just die of jealousy.'

'Poster, honey. It's a four-poster bed and I don't think you're s'posed to be fiddling with it. What do you s'pose that little red cord is draped there for? Besides...'

But Ruth Cohen had skipped off to molest another eighteenth century heirloom. Harry had never wanted to come on this trip. Haunted Heritage indeed. For four thousand dollars he could have stayed on the ranch and hired a spook or two to come jangle their chains or whatever they do.

Miss Kennedy was having trouble keeping her group together.

'If I can ask you all to refrain from wandering off. We've a lot to get through.'

She hitched her skirt round and made a promise to

herself to complain to her boss about the crabby uniforms and the boring tourists and the ropey coach and the leery driver. In fact, she was determined to tell him that the job was a big yawn and what he could do with it.

'OK, if we've all caught up now, can I draw your attention to these three magnificent window arches which look out over what used to be the main grounds? This lovely oil painting here…'

She glanced to the back of the group where three Japanese were squabbling over a camera. They looked up as she flicked withering contempt in their direction. They hastily put the camera away and stood like scolded schoolboys.

'…is by the celebrated artist, Sir Edward Hunter who, as a guest here, painted many views of Saxonby Abbey and the grounds and indeed, several portraits of members of the Hilchester family.'

'Honey, will you look at the lovely trees. We gotta get some of those for along the…'

Harry looked patiently at his wife.

'Ruthy, baby…look.'

He waved his arm in the direction of the window. A children's adventure playground, complete with rope slides and sand pits stood alongside a hamburger palace and a bouncy castle. A multi-story car park and a DIY/Garden Centre nestled under a giant glass dome.

'There ain't no trees, honey. See?'

'No, silly. In the painting.'

She motioned toward the painting. A silky sweep of lawn with a parade of pink-laden trees fell away from the black and white façade of the Abbey down to a willow-fringed sapphire lake.

Miss Kennedy droned on.

'This main part of the Abbey is Tudor and was completed in 1580, but the painting is a particularly fine example of how it would have looked in the eighteenth century.'

She swayed on down the woody corridor stopping in front of a dark portrait hanging in partial shadow.

'This...' she flung a bony white hand at the painting, '...is another example of Sir Edward's work. It is the only known portrait of Charles, the son of James Hilchester, the third Earl. Tragic.'

Harry looked at the painting. Green eyes gazed down from a pale face framed with a tumble of dark curls. A strikingly handsome face indeed.

'Tragic?' he asked.

The young couple had peeled away from the hubbub of the tour. He stroked her cheek. She parted her lips. They kissed softly, almost shyly. She loved him so much she wanted to die from the sweet pain of it all. She could still taste the champagne; hear the rustle of white silk. She'd wanted that day to last forever. Now she was drowning in the closeness of him and all she could think about was their future together, stretching out ahead of them. A lifetime.

'WILL you two come along?'

Miss Kennedy's shrill voice shattered the moment.

'Tea is being served in the Blue Drawing Room NOW, and I don't think you're actually supposed to be in there.'

Steve and Jacky Masters crept out from behind a display cabinet, giggling.

'Sorry,' mumbled Steve. 'Come on Mrs Masters...' he winked at his new wife. '...and button your blouse,' he whispered.

They followed Miss Kennedy, Jacky playfully grabbing a handful of Steve's left buttock.

The Blue Drawing Room was breathtakingly beautiful. Totally furnished in blue and cream with dark green drapes, its vaulted windows faced the west end of the lake. Harry perched on one of the wide sills and sipped his tea. The bustle of the tourist trade could not be seen from this side of the Abbey and he was having a quiet moment. The Reverend Barker had loosed himself momentarily from the grip of the Spooner sisters and approached Harry's corner.

'Mr Cohen. I see you have found yourself a little haven. Do you mind if I join you?'

'Hi there, your Reverendness. No, help yourself.'

Harry pointed to the other end of the sill.

'And it's Harry.'

'Thanks, Harry. I'm quite exhausted.'

Behind them, the drawing room rang to the clattering, chattering chink of tea cups and spoons. Voices rose and fell like a humming of bees on a sun-soaked afternoon. The Japanese had separated themselves from the others and were laughing and arguing, passing round guide books and photographs. The elderly Spooner sisters had captured Miss Kennedy and Ruth Cohen was, once again, on the wrong side of a red rope, poking a purple finger nail into some eighteenth century upholstery.

'So, how are you enjoying your English holiday, Harry?'

'Haunted Heritage, my eye.'

Harry put his cup down and reached for a plate of ginger cake from a nearby trolley.

'Cake, Rev?'

'Looks delightful. Don't mind if I do.'

The two munched silently for a moment.

'What were you hoping for? Ghouls and ghosties dripping from every chandelier? You don't see them gliding through walls…although…there is a definite atmosphere here. Don't you think?'

'Garbage, Rev, if you don't mind me saying so. Ruthie was keen to come. She loves all this ancient stuff. We don't got this at home and it makes her happy… and a happy Ruthie means a peaceful life.'

'Well, she should enjoy the rest of the tour. We've got the Tower of London tomorrow and Stratford on Saturday. I've been to both before, of course, but I had to come, having been roped in to escort half the parish.'

'You mean the Spooners. Don't they ever stop talking?' Frank Barker laughed.

'They've been telling everyone the story of the Abbey.'

'What actually happened? The book mentions a couple of murders but I haven't read it properly.'

Morag made her way to the stable block. She walked slowly. She wanted to make it last. The fluttering in her stomach moved all the way up to her chest. When she reached the edge of the kitchen garden, she glanced about. Mrs Chick was coming out of the pantry laden with wrapped cheeses. Round and splattered with flour, she looked exactly like one of her own cottage loaves. She looked up when she saw the girl. Morag busied herself pretending to pick peas.

'Morag, hen. Don't go eating all those, now. Leave some for the upstairs folk.'

Mrs Chick laughed to herself as she walked across the yard heading for the cold store.

It wouldn't always be like this. Hiding in corners. Watching. Waiting. Charles had told her to be patient. She was the one, but she would have to wait. Things were a little difficult at the moment. He'd have to talk to his father. The timing had to be right. The engagement to Lady Sarah, Lord Oakley's daughter, made things complicated. It would have to be dealt with carefully.

Gently.

She'd give him all the time he needed to sort things out. She would be the Countess one day. Charles had told her so.

As soon as Mrs Chick had disappeared into the cold store, Morag continued past the kitchens across the yard and into the stables. They were dark and thick with the scent of warm animals and leather. She waited a moment, leaned against a post and tried to slow her breathing. Her eyes grew accustomed to the gloom. Then she saw him. He was lying in the hay, waiting for her. She could see the green of his coat and the fall of dark hair against his cheek.

'Well…' continued Rev. Barker. '…they say he used to…er…dally with quite a few of the servant girls.'

'What a dog,' said Harry who was on his third slice of ginger cake.

'So, when they found them both dead, well…the scandal…the Earl was a broken man. He died the following year.'

'So, whodunit then Rev, as they say?'

'Well, the gardener hanged for it.'

'How come?'

'He made a full confession.'

'But why did he do it?'

'That is a very good question, Harry. A very good question indeed.'

Miss Kennedy was, once again, attempting to assemble her group. Harry hauled himself wearily to his feet.

'Where did she say we were going?'

'I wasn't listening, to tell you the truth, Harry. Sit back down for a minute, I've not finished my tea yet. We'll follow on in a moment. Perhaps we can get some shut-eye on the coach.'

Harry tried to imagine sleeping on the coach with Ruth wittering on. He closed his eyes.

'I really don't know why you people come on these trips at all.'

Harry's eyes flicked open. Miss Kennedy was standing over the newly-weds who had found a particularly soft chaise-longue and were entwined upon it.

'You could stay home and do that sort of thing.'

She couldn't even be bothered to be polite any more. The battle she'd been having with her skirt was over and the zip was facing south west.

'Watch out, Rev. The Wicked Witch has caught the love birds again.'

The increasingly unhappy little flock straggled along a corridor and down a flight of stone steps. They found themselves in a large room, empty except for a table in the centre. Several wooden cupboards were set into the walls. The floor was paved with flagstones and the temperature had dropped noticeably. Ruth Cohen shivered.

Miss Kennedy flipped the pages of her guide book.

'This is what would have been the kitchen,' she said.

'Surely this would have been the pantry,' volunteered Nancy Spooner.

'That's right,' said her sister. 'That's why it's so cold.'

Miss Kennedy breathed slowly and deeply, holding Nancy's glance and keeping it for a long moment.

'So, this would have been the KITCHEN,' she continued. The others looked at each other and remained silent.

'...and if we move out into the yard...'

Ruth was the first outside, glad of the late afternoon sunshine on her face.

Miss Kennedy stretched out her arms and fluttered her

fingertips.

'Gather round, gather round.'

They all dutifully clumped.

'The stable block over there...' she sighed, shifted her weight to her other hip and pointed.

Harry, who had caught up with the unhappy crew, imagined her in a sparkly leotard on a tacky TV game show pointing out Tonight's Star Prize. He fully expected to see an army of the living dead dance out of the stables, shaking gory locks to order.

'...is the scene of the actual murders. Screams can often be heard coming from the building.'

She wasn't going to mention that it was a deaf old bat from Bournemouth who thought she'd heard a scream a few years back. It was probably her hearing aid playing up.

'You've got twenty minutes. The coach leaves at five o'clock.'

She swivelled on her heel and walked quickly away.

Ruth bustled over to her husband.

'There you are. Where did you get to at tea? I'm going to see what they've got over there. You look tired, honey.' She pinched his cheeks.

He watched her wobble off on spiky heels in the direction of the souvenir shop. Rubbing his eyes and turning his baseball cap back-to-front, he made for the stables.

The Spooner sisters hijacked Frank Barker again, plonked him on a bench and proceeded to show him their snaps from their visit to Saxonby Abbey last year. And the year before that.

'We come every year,' they said. 'Such a sad little tale.'

The Japanese were taking pictures of each other, posing in front of the souvenir shop. The two families from Luton were arguing about whose turn it was to buy the ice cream and trying to explain to their six bawling children that there really was no time for one more go on the bouncy castle.

Jacky and Steve strolled across the yard, arms round each other.

'It's the saddest thing I've ever heard,' she said.

Her head was on his shoulder. He kissed her hair.

'Best not to go in then, love, if it upsets you.'

'No, I want to see where it happened. The romance of it all. Two young lovers, cruelly murdered where they lay, wrapped in each other's arms.'

'Romance? They were just having a bit of you know what.'

They looked at each other.

'What a cracking idea,' they said in unison.

He gripped the axe handle with a great sweating hand. The head of the axe dragged along the ground as he made his way up the garden. It was steep. He was breathing hard. He was glad the old oak was gone now. He should have done it last year. It had been blocking the light from the young fruit trees on the other side of the brook. Now, where was the girl?

He loved Morag dearly and since her mother died, she had looked after him well. Their life was not so bad, here on the estate. The Earl was a good man with a love of nature, often joining in with the planting; silk cuffs pushed back, dirt under his nails. Charles Hilchester, the Earl's son, was a different kettle of fish. Handsome and with a new fiancée in tow, the boy was a rogue. It was no secret that he had an eye for all the young girls on the staff. This raffish behaviour did not stop when the engagement to Lady Sarah was announced.

Just as well his own Morag had been brought up properly. She would never fall for any such nonsense. These things had a habit of getting out of hand. He'd seen it before. Upstairs folk should stay upstairs. Besides, Morag was only fifteen. If Charles Hilchester, or anyone else for that matter...

He flung the axe up and over his shoulder. Now, where was the girl?

He dropped her to the bare floor of the stable trying to imagine what it must have been like all those centuries ago. He could smell the horses. Feel the heat from their bodies. Now though, the floors were scrubbed clean. They'd probably turn them into extra tea rooms next season.

'No, Steve, you animal. Not here,' giggled Jacky.

'They're all off buying plastic fridge magnets. We've got the place to ourselves.'

Harry Cohen, sitting in the corner of the next stall, tried to pull his baseball cap over his ears and wished he was elsewhere. To jump up now would suggest he'd been eavesdropping or worse. Watching. The truth was, he'd been asleep and was woken by all the sighing. He sat tight.

Morag stood still and breathed lightly. She took a silent step forward and looked at her lover. Her eyes traced the curve of his cheek, the line of his mouth.

The axe was getting heavy now. He shifted it from his shoulder and carried it, cradling it. Absently fingering the blade. The back of the stable block was just ahead. Morag was sure to be there. He'd often seen her going in. He entered the sweet darkness. The Earl's mare was in the first stall. He moved past her and stopped, leaning against her flank. He listened.

Two people were in the next stall. Someone was breathing hard. The man was whispering. Morag's father knew the voice and loathing clawed at his body. His grip on the axe tightened and then he saw her. He saw his Morag on the other side of the stable. She stepped forward. She was watching something, her face contorted.

Charles Hilchester moved his shoulder, revealing the face of Lucy Hubble, the Countess's maid. She was beneath him. Her eyes were closed, her mouth open.

Morag stood watching, biting her bottom lip so hard her mouth filled with blood. Moving slowly, automatically, she picked up a hay fork, its twelve inch prongs reaching forward. Curving.

Another step forward. And another. Still they did not hear her. Morag's father remained rooted to the spot. She was running now, the fork held in front of her. As it passed through the bodies of both lovers, only the woman screamed.

Everybody stood still and looked at each other. Nancy Spooner jumped and clutched her chest. They all heard it. The scream came suddenly out of the sunshine and ripped round the yard. Nobody moved for a moment and then Reverend Barker began to run toward the stable door.

Harry was walking slowly out of the gloom. His eyes were wide. His arms were open, hands spread with palms upwards in a gesture of utter despair. Over his shoulder, Frank Barker could just make out the two lifeless figures pinned together. Skewered to the stable floor. The handle of a hay fork swaying gently.

ALPHA SEASON VIII.
2011-2012

Consolidating...
Following David's death the group needed someone to take over the function of coordinating activities. Christine had already stepped in on several occasions, including winding up the previous season, and she was invited to continue looking after the group. She agreed and set about familiarising herself with the details of planning and organising the season's activities. She chose to be known as the Group Coordinator (rather than any feminine form of David's title of Steward).

Alpha members have always been positive and willing to undertake tasks that enhance the Alpha experience, and Christine knew she could count on as much help as she needed. Olaf volunteered as her mentor and was always ready with advice.

Publication...
The Alpha Writers' Group had gained in prestige and self-esteem by the e-publication of the novella co-written by our members. There was mounting interest in repeating the success with other works written by the group.

Back in Season III David had launched and supervised the writing of a science fiction novella. It had been edited and proofread by David and Christine at the time and internally 'published' as a Word doc. for the benefit of members. We asked Rosemary if she'd do the necessary work of formatting it for e-publication. She agreed and *A Flower for Skalla* was e-published in March 2012.

And more...

Some members expressed their wish to see the anthology written as a tribute to David published on line where sales would benefit the Macmillan Cancer Research. We mulled it over, but with a total of about 3,000 words the Birth anthology alone didn't warrant e-publishing. However, the Alpha Group has never been idle and there was the music anthology we'd written in Season IV: six stories totalling nearly 8,000 words. If we added the sonnets that had been such a success for one of the season's challenges we'd have a rich and varied anthology that we could be very proud of.

The *Birth | Music | Sonnets* anthology was edited, proofread and polished by Rosemary and Christine. Rosemary formatted it for e-publication.

The season's usual activities continued while the progress of our publications caused the occasional flutter of excitement.

Alpha Season VIII, Challenge 2:

Challenge 2 had the following brief:
'Imagine you're a reporter at ONE of the following. Write a piece conveying some 'immediacy' of the event. Either a purely factual piece, or 'opinion'. Make it journalism: in the days before radio, TV, etc, you're writing for people who weren't actually there. (No anachronisms).

1. The Salem Witch Trials, Massachusetts, North America (1692)

2. The opening of the Liverpool to Manchester railway, 15 September 1830

3. The 1913 Derby where suffragette Emily Wilding was trampled to death

250 - 350 words'

The winning entry, written by Geoff:

The Witch Report: October 1692
Spook Spoofery at the Salem Trials!

Nineteen innocent Salem residents hanged by witch-hunting courts! Fie on such fools who manifest the evil they claim to eradicate! How dare they do the Devil's work for us!

Remember 1688, dear Witches, when Salem Village's richest farmers, the Putnams, claimed higher holiness than the fishing faction of Salem Town by concocting a splinter congregation under Rev. Samuel Parris.

The perk-plucking Parris, mired in an expense claim scandal, sank deeper when his slave, Tituba, lured his daughter and niece into 'freakish' fortune-telling and wishy-washy witchcraft. Their cranky behaviour saw them pronounced 'bewitched'. A dog fed on rye-meal mixed with the girls' urine replicated their banal spasms, prompting them to name Tituba their witch-tormentor.

Holy worriers jumped on the bandwagon accusing elderly lapsed church-goer, Sarah Osborne, and homeless beggar, Sarah Good, of witchcraft, as if two such wimpish losers could possess the gushing venom of true Witches! Puritanical paranoia jailed all three to 'appease God's wrath'.

Ann Putnam cried 'Witchcraft!' at elderly Rebecca Nurse's hovering spectre for 'pinching and torturing' her.

Martha Corey allegedly 'spooked' her as did ex-minister George Burroughs, 'Leader of the Salem Coven'. What nonsense! And what an insult to the true holder of that grand title!

The final tally of jailed suspects in May was around 200. 'Spectral evidence' which incriminated them was later declared unreliable, local intelligentsia claiming the Devil could perform evil through an innocent person. No kidding!

This failed to prevent the hanging of Bridget Bishop (a mere dabbler!) on June 10th for allegedly sticking pins into 'poppets' of her victims. Poppets?! How twee!

Eighteen more souls were sacrificed on pure whim. Good on Giles Corey, though, for ignoring the court's questions last month while they piled boulders on his chest until he died by crushing. With such commitment, plus a dash of our own slaughterous evil, he could have been a worthy comrade!

As any self-respecting Witch will confirm, these ludicrous trials betray utter ignorance of authentic demonic witchcraft. So, let's poke the Putnams with some real Witchcraft for our November issue!

This Alpha Decade contribution was inspired by the Season VIII brief:

Victorian Railways: Excursion Ticket to Change
Written by Olaf

Mention the nineteenth century to twenty-first century residents and they'll think of clouds of steam typifying the Industrial Revolution and that will lead them on to the railways, the Great Exhibition of 1851 and probably Queen Victoria. They'll perhaps put these together and say,

"That's History. Let's get on with the Now."

However, the achievements of the nineteenth century affect us all in many ways. Big locomotives may now be romantic curiosities, and the Crystal Palace thought of as a football club. Queen Victoria will be remembered as a long reigning monarch, and steam is what comes out of the kettle when you're making a cup of tea.

Yet if we think back to the beginning of the nineteenth century, the scientific and industrial world was experimenting with steam engines of various kinds. Our world was transforming, and men and animals could no longer provide the power needed to drive machinery to do repetitive and simple jobs. Hitherto, what mechanical means there was consisted of a small amount by windmills to grind corn while running water provided more reliable sources, but only where streams existed or water diverted through leets. Steam power had little in the way of constraints in position: power could be provided where it was needed. No wonder it was an attractive proposition.

Where steam was used, whether in mining in Cornwall or in manufacturing in the Midlands and North, the beginning of the century saw growth in output. There was an economy in costs, but far from reducing the labour needed, it became an attractive investment opportunity with expansion and a need for more labour to maximise the use of this manufacturing capacity. As a result, the wages paid to men began to rise, health began to improve and the mortality of children dropped.

Alongside this general adopting of steam power to help manufacturing, there was a need to shift large and heavy volumes of raw materials and products. Concentration of research shifted to creating significant mobile sources of power, initially to pull wagons of spoil or ore. The concept of moving people instead of materials was never far removed and various initiatives were seen all over the country, with George Stephenson and Isambard Brunel providing much in the way of design and development.

The first scheduled passenger train service between Liverpool and Manchester started in 1830, but was accompanied by a disaster: a Minister of the Crown was run over by an engine, and died. This unfortunate incident did not in any way deter development, although for some years travel by rail was viewed as a method of transport for the better off. Even though fares were much lower than using stagecoach, the ordinary population still had little need for travel, still less the appetite or financial resources to do so.

Queen Victoria seems to have shown little interest in scientific and industrial progress, but her consort, Prince Albert did. He was highly impressed by the products that were being made, especially in Britain by the improved industrial progress, but also around the world by more traditional means. He was the essential driving force behind the idea to hold a Great Exhibition in London, far bigger than had been held in any other country. It received the go-ahead, and a competition for a suitable (temporary) building was held at the start of 1850. The Glass structure was popularly named the 'Crystal Palace', and was built and erected in 9 months: it was itself one of the attractions of British achievement.

These were the ingredients for success: a superbly attractive exhibition, demonstrating British ability to 'make it' with rail transport to get people there. It was a great success by any assessment, yet perhaps the greatest achievement was social progress in the following half-century. This has to be assessed against a background of private investment in progressing steam research, private investment in modernising factories and in establishing railways (although they had to receive the approval of the Government) and the Great Exhibition was a private enterprise. Social progress in the nineteenth century was never the result of governmental planning.

The Great Exhibition, opened in May 1851 and remained open for 6 months. During that time, no fewer than 6 million visited the exhibition, while the population of the whole country was around 15 million. For a true perspective on such a number, the Millennium 2000 exhibition in London was open for a whole year, and gained 6 million visitors, while the population of Britain exceeded 60 million, and our transport systems are well developed.

It is a straightforward step to deduce from this that the railway system in Britain was well developed as it was the only realistic transport system that could take people to London from the provinces for the purpose of visiting the Exhibition. Most of the railway companies – even from as far afield as York, saw the opportunities for business. In fact, railway building in Britain had proceeded apace in the decade before 1850, and we had the most developed rail transport in the world. No visitor, either from London, the provinces or abroad, could fail to be convinced by the ease of transport.

There were other factors contributing to the success. Manufacturing firms were being a little more considerate towards their workers. Although the six-day week was still the norm, a significant number allowed their employees time off (probably a day) to visit the Exhibition. The railway companies saw the opportunity and began to run 'excursion trains' – that is special trains not timetabled.

This had been tried – without much success – before, but this was an extraordinary opportunity. A special train could almost be guaranteed to have every seat filled, and the fare asked was much lower than any cheap day return.

Humans, like animals, have an inbuilt aspiration to explore. Until the mid-century, that desire had to be satisfied by walking or – for the better-off – on horseback. Yet here was the chance to travel and explore and seek new avenues of entertainment and relaxation for minimal cost.

The employment situation in the country also meant that the difference between the earnings of an employee and his costs left a surplus, albeit small, in the household budget. This disposable income could allow them some leisure pursuit, although go-away holidays were largely unknown.

Although the railway companies had been offering cheap day return tickets and excursion tickets before the Great Exhibition, they soon realised that there was a real and lasting market for excursion trips. Until that time, Exhibitions had tended to be local affairs in towns, with animals and human freaks, but not collections of items on a bigger scale. Likewise, the Exhibition itself showed that there was a source of income, albeit on a smaller scale so that one town could have an exhibition for a day.

So the idea of linking train excursions with trips to the seaside, spectacles or smaller exhibitions grew, and the first really successful attempt was made by Thomas Cook, towards the end of 1851.

The demand for excursion tickets grew, although there was resistance at first against travel on a Sunday. Excursion tickets were created for all kinds of events. Sea bathing, wrestling matches, ox roasting and horse racing, which was beginning to enjoy an improved attendance. There were however, some events which do not reflect so well from the present day. Excursions to public hangings were not uncommon, and were well patronised. It is on record that for one public hanging at Bodmin gaol, the excursion tickets sold at Wadebridge, just ten miles away, amounted to more than half the population of the town. An initiative to permit ladies to travel at a reduced price was abandoned when examples of trans-gender dressing meant that the rule could not be enforced.

The attraction of excursion trains grew, and soon, such trains were chartered by specific groups. Temperance groups were not uncommon, although on more than one occasion an excursion to Skegness resulted in the town being 'drunk dry'. Works outings followed later and for a time were a vital link in the relationship between management and workers.

Railway companies were capital intensive in respect of the rolling stock and the permanent way, and profit margins depended largely on passenger numbers. These were generally somewhat over-estimated when promising dividends for shareholders, and the railway companies were always looking for additional traffic. Excursion trains were well supported in number, but even in the period of the Great Exhibition, the profit margins were surprisingly narrow, as prices had been cut too far.

Many seaside towns provided termini at the end of the line, and where there were facilities of sea and sand, they became focal points for excursion trains, and they owe their growth to the ease of access by rail. Blackpool is the prime example – a wonderful day out opportunity for the population of the cotton towns of Lancashire: indeed so many trains ventured towards the town that it was common practice to link them together into a single unit.

The longest such train involved joining five individual trains together, carrying a total of 10,000 passengers – which the station at Blackpool couldn't handle.

The habit of various works forming their own football teams thrived from the mid-century. At first, the matches would be relatively local, but as the ease of transport grew, they formed into bigger and better units: in this way the first teams of the National Football League were able to compete against each other, and gain revenue from travelling supporters. The recognition of Saturday afternoon recreation led to the government establishing the five-and-a-half day week in 1875, although it had become an acceptable practice before then.

Eventually, the joys of days at the sea became weeks at the sea for those families that could afford it, and the education gained through excursions proved its value. The importance of rail travel to the sea is nowhere better illustrated than by the curious episode of a highly 'atmospheric' painting by Norman Garstin for the Royal Academy Exhibition in 1881, entitled 'The rain, it raineth every day'. After the exhibition, Garstin presented it to the Town Council. They accepted it, but stowed it away in the vaults, for they considered that it would damage the town's image now that the railway had recently reached Penzance. It is now on display in the town's principal gallery, where it is admired.

Excursion trains have now disappeared – there is very little room to accommodate them on heavily used tracks, and the rail transport system even further from being profitable. The equivalent of excursion trains has now shifted to low-cost flights, with tour operators arranging all kinds of excursions to foreign regions, and many of those regions are capitalising on their quotas of sunshine as well as sea and sand.

Author's Note: This article and the analysis it contains was inspired by the book "Away for the Day" by Arthur and Elizabeth Jordan, obtained as a publisher's remainder for £1.

ALPHA SEASON IX.
2012-2013

Amateur Dramatics...
We're an email group of writers who only ever meet in the virtual sphere of cyber space. The idea of launching Alpha Writers into the realm of amateur dramatics for a pantomime based on Cinderella may seem quite unrealistic. However, in the wonderful world of the imagination everything is possible.

The following account is from Olaf's annual report of our activities published in *Writers' News:*

> *An additional activity was the creation of a fictional Amateur Dramatic Society. Members described characters, and some of these were chosen as the object of our writing endeavours. Three particular aspects of the activity were featured – the committee meeting, rehearsals and scenery & props. Members contributed stories describing the activity within the Society, these being subject to critique, proofreading and comment by other members. What emerged was a very amusing and well-written account of scenes experienced in a (worldwide?) dramatic society. Those of us who have been members of such a society might quail at the collection of extraordinary characters. There are always some, but this many?*

Paperback Publications...
Following on from our e-book range of Alpha books we

now moved one step further.

Rosemary had perfected her technical skills to the superior, professional level. She added her extensive business experience and set up her own publishing company. Print-on-demand paperback publication was included in her range of services, and for the Alpha Writers' Group this was like a very lucky windfall.

Rosemary published our three Alpha books on Alfie Dog Fiction, Amazon and Smashwords in May 2013; available in e-book and paperback format.

Every one of the Alpha books has an excellent front cover illustration which Margie's daughter, a graphic artist, provided in consultation with the group.

Alpha Season IX, Challenge 2:

Our challenges continued to stir our creative talents into action and Challenge 2 had the following brief:

'Describe an event/happening/occasion which you have experienced during the last three months, relating to the part of the world in which you live (within about 100km/60 miles). The important thing is to **convey something about your environment**, but try to avoid a travelogue style. 300 words.'

The winning entry was written by Chris:
It was a red white blue, gold and purple day. It was a day of pageantry and flageantry, and it wound through our busy rural village like a Chinese New Year dragon. A dragon may be a mythical creature but it looks no more odd than the alpacas which are farmed in these parts; unlike the alpacas, our dragon formed a slow crocodile procession

which snaked its way through the village in honour of a little old lady, who has held the bridal and reigns of monarchy in this land for sixty years.

The village is the village; the people are The People; the queen is The Queen. The Queen is The People; the people are the village, and always have been. The dragon crocodile smiled a sixty-year smile and waved flags. We, its scales, moved (sometimes in rhythm) to the ragged oompah of an amateur marching band of villagers, while majorettes of all shapes, age, and sizes dipped, twirled, and high stepped along the High Street.

Did we all feel united in joy and happiness and memories? Probably not. But it was an extra holiday, and no-one really minded: certainly not the local publicans who had to stay open, nor even our Republicans who sat all afternoon in the pubs raising their glasses to no-one in particular.

'Twas brillig and the Jubilee
Did gyre and gimble down our way
All mimsy were the villagers
And the mome raths outpoured and grabed a barbecue, a disco, a talent show, and a concert or two, and everyone was happy for a while.

The following Alpha Decade contribution was vaguely inspired by this brief:

The Rundle Ruins.
Written by Rose.

Nor less, I trust
To them I may have owed another gift,
Of aspect more sublime; that blessed mood,

In which the burthen of the mystery,
In which the heavy and the weary weight
Of all this unintelligible world,
Is lighted.
William Wordsworth

The long dirt road into town morphs into cobblestone. The neighborhoods are tiny rows along the banks of the river. The main street leads northwest bending towards the southwest. Farmland, ranches, homesteads, all feed towards the main street. The old hospital, the doctor's residency, a nurse's routine and the terminal days of the elderly exist in between.

Each day begins with the milk run, the mail accompanied by the rumble of two great rivers that form the delta. It ends with the ringing of a brass bell. Three sandstone buildings stand on a large acreage of land to the east of the Elbow, a small slip of a river that cuts a smooth angle into the landscape. The river runs red under a flame colored sky. Streaks of amber, orange, pink and red fade to purple. A wagon hauling milk travels along the river. Two draft horses pull a wagon full of empty milk containers. Aluminium and glass chime together until the wagon stops.

Norman Bartholemue Mortinger is 77 years old. He is dying of cancer. Which type, he can't quite articulate to himself any more. He just accepts that this is what is. He waits by the picket fence, outside the main entrance to the three buildings. You can count twelve chimney stacks over red-shingled rooftops on a good day. This morning the red sky flows into the roof top. The sandstone bleeds red from roof top to ground. The windows of the hospice ward reflect the rage of the sky.

At night the old man sees the sandstone as dark blue, reflecting a cold winter moon. This morning the stone work absorbs the colorful sky around it. The old man always takes his walk at this time. He's been waiting to pass for four long months. The wait and the routine drag on. Every morning he brings the milk in. It is his reason to wake up.

Every morning he hears the music of the glass and aluminium milk containers. He hears the chime of them in his sleep. Every morning the sounds call him out, the wagon and the morning sun. The nursing staff at the hospice are surprised by this daily miracle.

At the end of each day the bell in the courtyard of the hospice is rung by the staff. Each clang of the bell signifies those who finally pass on into death. An epidemic caused the bell to ring eight times when he first arrived at the hospice. At night the wind shifts the heavy brass, the soft whisper clanging carries towards his ward. Sometimes when the bell chimes so softly, a patient sighs in contentment and passes on.

That is the trick, Norman thought. Wait for the soft chime and drift peacefully onwards. Wake up each morning. Deliver the milk from the wagon. Wait for the next sunrise. Waiting, always waiting. He feels more like a man drifting from something he loves dearly, away and towards a thing he never intended. He shakes his head. His thoughts often drift into half remembered fancies. Long forgotten in his youth, but now suddenly so important as he feels himself approaching death.

The hospice staff are as immutable as these thoughts that he shakes off daily. Half remembered ideas about the women he's known. He wishes he still knew a few of them. He remembers with a smile the whispered promises he always made, then broke. He remembers that half built idea of family. The house that was never filled with children. Another reincarnated lifetime, he has another shot at it once his current life expires.

He stands now before the sandstone archway to the hospice ward. Twelve or so glass milk bottles chime with each of his steps. He stops, looks back at the sky.

The pink, red and amber streaks in the sky turn the milk the color of pamplemousse, the pink color he adores, and the tart taste he hates. He pours sugar over the tartly offensive grapefruit. Grapefruit is like the tart taste of regret that continuously haunts him. The sting of what he should have done. He should have kept a journal.

He should have accomplished many things. Nothing ever materialized in any form that satisfied the answer to the question about meaning in his life.

He expected the milk to curdle in the pink light, as angry as it was this morning.

Norman shuffles forward, down the hallway towards the nursing station that is the entrance to the hospice ward. He sees Sidney, a nurse in her mid-forties working in the hospice. She is sitting at the station desk, waiting to buzz him. She smiles with pity as he approaches. He completes his task of delivering the milk to its destination. He is simply in transit.

The nurse smiles indulgently at Norman as he shuffles forward. She buzzes him through the cage, into the receiving area of the hospice ward. She eyes him; Norman's survived another night. Surprising, the Doctor says. The Nurse knows that Norman is there for other reasons. Doctors knew little of practicality, in her opinion. Motivation is the key to survival. Or, she thought, in the case of those who choose to prolong their stay. Norman, in her opinion, had unfinished business.

The nurse twirls the ring on her left hand. The small alexandrite gem stone feels like a dumbbell on her finger.

Her routine is this; brush aside the stray curly black hair into a regulated bun. Slide the ring onto the ring finger of her left hand. Go to work. Complete the daily routine of helping others in the twilight of their lives. Go home. Make dinner. Remove the gem stone. Place it oh-so-carefully beside the picture of him; the picture of her husband smiling, with a black silk band around the base.

Sleep. Rinse. Repeat.

With a sense of bitterness, Sidney twirls the ring again. The lives of the exception rarely cross hairs with those who live a normal life, with normal problems on normal days. However the routine works out, the routine itself is a reason to keep in the game.

Yes, she thought, her routine keeps her from giving in to her grief. Her grief for a husband who died too early.

Hospitals are notorious for routine. Without routine a hospital would cease to function, in her opinion.

She watches Norman shuffle around the corner into the hospice ward. If the old man knows he never lets on. Routine really is the medicine against a terminal illness. Routine allows you the momentary illusion that death is preventable.

Sidney remembers a woman in her mid-twenties. The woman grew up on the farm. Their exceptional doctor diagnosed her. A week later she landed in room 214, ward 4, with TB. Funny thing, her family wrote her off. TB is a thing no healthy girl has. She'd gone within a week.

Funny, how the stone and the sky know to neglect the moods within the ward. How detached she's become, she thinks. The passing of each day is so natural. Yet she works each day in a place engulfed in a war against time.

The oversized brass bell in the courtyard rings out in the evening. Rarely a day passes without the chime, without the body count. She stopped hearing the bell, she knows that, after the fifth year. It was the year her husband died.

On days when the bell does not toll, the silence is the sound of a canon.

The winter is long this year. Nothing grows. The life of the natural world is not present around the hospice.

The blood that bleeds from the sky, into the roof, down into the sandstone does not leach into the patients. She remembers the year of the yellow fever. The number of children is the worst fact about the outbreak. The tally of the dead each day fell to her to count. The daily toll of the bell for each child that passed was rung by her hand.

Her longest set of chimes is eight. After that day she refused to ring the bell. She also stopped hearing the bell. Both are related in her mind. It is also the day the Doctor's sister died.

The nursing staff at the ward monitor each child every day. The daily routine grew to include each child growing weaker and succumbing to the illness that spread through the community. It had been difficult to endure.

Yet endure she did.

Of all the children admitted that year to the ward, three lived. One of these children is now the resident Doctor. He works in the Hospice center, where he and his sister were treated so many years ago.

Sidney thinks of how he looks now, Alfie. Dr. Alfred Arnould, a Doctor nowadays. Dr. Arnould is a tall man in his early thirties with a premature silver streak beginning at his temples. He has kind brown eyes beneath large eyebrows on a prominent forehead. His hair parts down the middle, kept in check by a comb always present in the left pocket of his jacket. He has a face with a road map of laughter drawn out of the creases at the eyes to the deepened dimple by his mouth. He shuffles a few feet forward, shoulders turned inwards, out of habit.

To her surprise the Doctor remembers her. Alfred is his first name. During his time there, she called him Alfie. 'My, has Alfie grown!' is her first thought every morning when he arrives at the hospice. The first dialogue between them was "You're the one who rang the bell for Sarah. Thank you."

As a nurse, you push the routine, the daily list of elements that need to happen, for the doctors in residence to do their jobs. These things need to happen. Once the Doctor let it be known he'd come through that terrible time as a child the nurse looked through the logs. There he was, age 9, written in her neat longhand into the books. He'd been admitted with his sister. He'd been discharged without her. It is the custom for Doctors to offer a few words of wisdom to the nursing corps. Sidney remembers his starting words.

> 'If solitude, or fear, or pain, or grief
> Should be thy portion, with what healing thoughts
> Of tender joy wilt thou remember me'
> *William Wordsworth*

Those words move her every day. The door is suddenly in shadow. A familiar shadow. 'Think of the devil and he shall appear,' Sidney thinks.

Alfie, or Dr. Arnould, walks toward her station from the doorway. She obediently buzzes him through. A small friendly smile appears on his face as he passes.

'Good Morning, Dr. Arnould.' she says.

'Good Morning, Sidney,' he says.

The Doctor remembers the staff who'd helped him and his sister. Regardless of the outcome, he felt indebted to them. Despite his own feelings of fear, pain, solitude or grief, he recalls the time that benefitted him and his sister the most. When surrounded by strangers, the routine and predictability is a comfort to those who face the unknown.

Doctor Arnould looks at his chart for the day. His office is to the left of the Nurses' station, a subtle doorway just before the receiving area of the hospice ward. His desk is in gentle disarray. A few files here, a few pens litter the desk drawer. The chart has Norman front and center for his morning rounds.

The 'Good Doctor' Norman calls him. 'Herr Doctor', at times, when the day hasn't gone that well. He asks the nurse if Norman is German. 'No,' she replies simply. The nurse is practical. The patients are not. He knows the nurses via the patients at times. A comment here or a roll of the eyes there. These acts are never forgotten, even as the nurse disappears around the corner. Out of sight but never out of mind. At least not his mind, anyway.

The Doctor is terrible with names. He simply moves from one chart to the next, noting the day's events in chemical dosages. The nurses remember names and assign nicknames as appropriate. He remembers signs, symptoms of terminal illnesses. He does not know the secret to life. He knows every threat to human physiology. He knows how to keep a body alive long after that which defines life, the soul, checks out forever.

The night shift ends shortly before he arrives in the morning. Rarely does he see the nights pass as the patients and staff do. He had had enough of the nights there, when he was a sick child. The bell, he swore it chimed at night by means of a supernatural volition. The metal voice of the dead or dying whispers over the courtyard, over the military rank and file tulips, to his office window.

He remembers a tough night, years ago, when the sun rose red in the morning hours. That night he dreamed. There was a garden between two buildings, a large calm expanse of neat flower beds and solid wooden benches. A small fountain; a girl in copper turned green, poured water from a vase into a pool. Birds converged around the water. They flew in between the water and the bird feeder. The bell stood just beyond the small fountain. His sister stood behind the bell, pulled the chord. The bell tolled once and jarred him out of sleep.

Disoriented he had fumbled in the dark, not knowing the time or place. Not the bedroom in the house in Rouleauville. Not the bedroom in the homestead on his grandfather's ranch. He was in the hospice ward, a small boy of 9. A shared, cold dark place where he'd only known life for a few weeks. The nurse, Sidney, had walked by his bed at that moment. He watched, later, as Sidney rang the bell for his sister that morning. He stopped hearing the bell that day.

The routine is a small comfort to him now. The competent nurses perform daily necessary tasks. The staff help to relieve the terminal mood of the hospice ward.

When the Doctor walks to the acreage of land where the hospice is, he crosses a ridge of land. Over the ridge he looks towards the Elbow river, the Bow river, the path over the ridge provides a spectacular view of a developing city.

A small city, but it is his and his family's. To the west are the mountains. To the east there are endless golden wheat fields. The sky engulfs the city in Chinook arches of clouds from end to end. The colors of the landscape amaze him every morning. He imagines the ranchers watching apprehensively as the city creeps closer, over to the west of the Glenmore reservoir.

The Doctor walks after dinner in the garden of the hospice. He watches as the shadows grow, dark forms lengthen as the light is lost. Inky outlines against the grass and dirt of the garden stretch and grow larger than the buildings.

When the moon is full, the shadows are incomplete specters that morph into one unrecognizable shape; they pass overhead until the sun chases the moon beyond the horizon, where it disappears.

All this begins, and ends, with the tolling of a bell.

ALPHA SEASON X.
2013-2014

Thesis...

Our common interest is writing. Over the years we've developed an Alpha routine that allows us to explore writing from different angles. The challenges give us the opportunity to practise our skills in a variety of genres. The Log provides a platform for sharing our personal writing experiences and our efforts to find outlets for our work in the outside world. During Season X we also created a showcasing slot. We had previously dabbled in showcasing some of our work in an informal way. For Season X Clare volunteered to organise it on a regular basis. She collected the pieces to be showcased and sent them out to the group at regular intervals for comment and critique. It proved a great success. On top of that we often had email exchanges about subjects of major or minor interest that somehow cropped up.

Sally and Rosemary re-designed our web site, gave it a thorough overhaul and transferred it to Wordpress. Rosemary offered to be in charge of keeping it up to date, posting the season's events as they happened as well as general information about the Alpha Group.

Everyone willingly took on tasks and contributed to the various slots. As a result we could always look forward to Alphadays with a rich supply of writerly treats.

Antithesis...
We're a motley group of people with as many individual quirks and convictions as there are members. We're scattered to the four corners of the globe and our writing spans everything from fiction to non-fiction and poetry, picking up a spread of genres from romance to fantasy and everything in between.

We have had the occasional member leaving the group because they were expecting something that we don't provide. But they're few and far between. Some move on because of other commitments and we benefit from the fresh input of new members which ensures that our group never grows stale.

Synthesis...
Our way of running the group works on all levels. We thoroughly enjoy the company of other writers which allows us to escape the lonely isolation of that (in)famous garret. There is no teaching involved. Every member contributes their particular skills and interests for the benefit of the whole group. Some members have met in 'real life'. It doesn't often happen but when we're told of these encounters it's always a pleasure for the rest of us to hear how it went. However, our significant encounters are of the virtual kind. We bond with our fellow members and when personal tragedies affect one of us we rally together to offer support and sympathy in whichever way we can. Happy events also cause a ripple of pleasure that we all share. The common factor – the great synthesiser – is our writing, and writing is a very personal business. A writer writes from the heart and we're all aware of it. We respect and admire this as we share our writing experiences in the stimulating company of like-minded people.

The one-year experiment has completed a full decade of delights for writers. It shows no signs of slowing down... if anything Alpha appears to get even more vigorous with age.

For a number of seasons Alpha had indulged in the Seven Deadly Sins as the theme for one of our challenges. This time the brief was as follows:

Alpha Season 10, Challenge 9:

'Write on the theme of **Jealousy**. The title, of your choosing, is not included in the word count. Include in your entry, as seamlessly as possible, the words **"departures", "travel", "smell"**. No variations on these words. Max. 300 words.'

The winning entry was written by Stephen:
A Visit to the Opera

There are those for whom departures from normal, civilised behaviour are unforgiveable and there are those who regard the unconventional as normal or even exciting.

Karlheinz Schmalkalden was not normal. Not in the sense you or I would regard as normal. Nothing perturbed him, no-one annoyed him. Through the worst of abuse he would emerge with a smile of obvious forgiveness. Indeed, he would look as if he were still savouring the enticing scent of a damask rose even as he responded – with a gentle tone- to his wife Birgitte's perpetual condemnation of what she called his congenitally uninteresting personality.

Birgitte never addressed Karlheinz without looking as if he had left a foul smell of something rotten in her nostrils. They had both come to accept this pattern for their lives.

No-one, therefore, least of all Birgitte, supposed Karlheinz capable of the extreme jealousy he displayed that evening when he and Birgitte decided to travel to the opera at Bochum to see Der Rosenkavalier. When, in the foyer of the theatre, Birgitte smiled, fluttered her eyelids and positively cooed in response to the elderly gentleman who took her hand, kissed it and remarked how charming she looked, Karlheinz did not just burn with jealousy, he exploded

As the Bochumer Zeitung put it, Karlheinz became puce, shouted at the old gentleman, declared him to be a disgusting old lecher, struck him down with a single blow, scattering beautifully dressed ladies on all sides, and ushered his wife firmly into the auditorium and their seats.

Poor Birgitte's mind was in turmoil throughout the whole of Act One.

Then she smiled. He was jealous. The boring old fool was really jealous. Maybe she had misjudged him these thirty years past.

They must make the effort to go to the opera more often.

The following Alpha Decade contribution was vaguely inspired by the brief:

It's Time...
Written by Geoff.

Ethel is feisty. It isn't that she doesn't suffer fools gladly. She doesn't suffer them at all.

"I've not got enough time left on this planet to waste it with nincompoops," she'll say as she dismisses people with a derisory wave of the hand.

Her daughter Cathy tries to remind her that such rudeness in others would have appalled her years ago.

"I dare say, love, but we had standards then. This is not the England I was brought up in and fought for. My word, no. This is a quagmire, more like. I'm just adapting to it, the same as everybody else. Your generation has a lot to answer for, my girl."

Steering her mother away from the minefield of hobbyhorses, Cathy reminds her that it's her 87th birthday.

"Don't rub it in. I hope you're not planning some sort of party. I hate parties. I've got nobody left anyway, just a street full of widows. Isn't that typical? We slog away all our lives pandering to our menfolk and their every whim. Then just when they retire and are finally going to be of some use around the place, they're dead. Selfish buggers."

"Come on, Mum, Dad didn't know he'd got a dodgy ticker. He was always longing for his retirement so he could work on the house and take you places."

"Cathy, when it came down to it, your father wasn't here for me. He let me down."

"What are you talking about? He was a wonderful husband and father. You don't hear anybody else slagging off their late husbands. You're getting so hard."

"It's a hard world dear, I'd have thought you would have learned that by now. Your husband didn't even have the decency to die before he abandoned you!"

"Listen, Mum, I'm not getting into all this with you. Jenny should be arriving soon so let's create a slightly more hospitable atmosphere."

"She's all right is that daughter of yours, I'll give you that. How she turned out so well I'll never know."

"Thanks, Mum. That's a kind thought."

"Is she seeing anybody or is she making the most of her life?"

"You can ask her yourself when she gets here. If she ever

does. She said she'd be here at 4 o'clock. She must have been held up. She's usually very reliable."

"Has she not got one of those mobile phones that's giving everybody cancer these days?"

"That's never been proved, Mum. I expect her battery's low, that'll be it."

"Poverty of modern invention, that's what it is, dear."

"Jesus, don't you ever let up?"

"Hey! No need for blasphemy, Catherine."

"Thank God you still believe in something."

"If I didn't have my faith I wouldn't have anything."

"So we can all thank the Lord for your charitable good nature."

The doorbell rings loudly, causing Ethel's heart to skip a beat.

"Dear, oh dear, I thought He'd come for me then. That bell needs fixing. It's been too loud since October 1977."

Cathy opens the front door. Her daughter is standing on the step, beaming, arm in arm with a rather smart young man who, for the moment, is oozing self-confidence.

Jenny steps forward.

"Hi Mum. Hi, Gran. Sorry we're late, we overslept. Gran, this is Russell."

Russell grasps Ethel's hand.

"Such a pleasure to meet you, Mam."

Ethel's smile is more of a grimace.

"You American?"

"Sure am, Mrs Wood."

"No wonder you're late, Jenny. Americans! Late for the war, late for their own funeral!"

"Steady on, Mum," said Cathy.

Jenny laughs at the awkwardness.

"There you go, Russell. Told you she'd love you at first

sight."

"Allow me, madam, to apologise on behalf of the government and people of the United States of America, for entering the Second World War so late in the day and with such arrogance."

"How dare you talk down to me, young man."

"I wasn't talk…"

"Now you listen to me. I don't know if you're being naïve American or smart arse American, though I fear they're both born of the same inferiority complex."

"Jeez!"

"And I won't have cursing in this house."

"Happy birthday, Mrs Wood! I'm delighted to meet you. I've heard a lot…"

"Bullshit!"

"Excuse me?"

"I said bullshit, young man. I've decided to talk up to you, for the sake of my very dear grand-daughter."

"Isn't somebody gonna offer me a cup of tea? That's what you Brits do in moments of extremis, isn't it?"

"We English can't simply be labelled Brits, young man. I don't know how long you've been cohabiting with my grand-daughter, but she obviously hasn't got very far with you. Shame on you, Jenny Weedon."

Jenny puts her arms around Ethel and kisses her.

"Happy birthday, Gran. Shall I put your present over here and start a pile?"

"I hope you haven't got any big surprises lined up. That'll kill me off right there. Remember Hilda Hepple whose son arranged a surprise birthday party for her 80th? She keeled over and died when she realized who all those crinkly faces were, lined up round her front room. You'd better not be dragging up people from the past, not that there are any left."

"Your grannie sure has balls, Jen!"

"That, young man, is something I've never been accused of, though I have scared off men much uglier than you."

"Hey! I'll take that as a compliment."

"Take it any way you like ... what's your name? Russell? Anyway, why haven't you got the kettle on yet? Jenny, you need to get your men under control, otherwise you'll end up like your mother."

You're awfully short for an American, Russell. Where was your family from?"

"Well, my name is Schneider…"

"Schneider!"

"Sure. Does that mean something to you?

"Only that it's German!"

"That's right."

"You can't seriously be telling me that my only grandchild is sleeping with the enemy."

"Hey, Gran, that's enough!"

"Mum, you're being way too weird. I'm sorry, Russell. My mother's …"

"How dare you apologise for me, Catherine…"

"It's OK, Mrs Wood. Let me explain. My grandfather escaped from Germany as Chancellor Hitler was starting to make his evil mark on Europe. I'm no more the enemy than my grandfather was. I know you've suffered a lot at Germany's hands…"

"Suffered? I fought against them with my own hands. So did my dear husband. Our lives were ruined by Germany."

"They weren't ruined, Mum", says Cathy. "You describe the war as the best years of your life. You cherish them."

"I cherish your father's memory, that's what. If he were here today…"

"If he were here today, Gran, he'd tell you what a great job you did in building a happy, closely knit family."

"Closely knit! Look at us! We won a World War for this! Look what's happened to us. We have nothing."

Cathy gets up and leaves the room, shaking her head.

"Gran, we have each other. Don't be silly."

Ethel falters as her tears well up. She pulls a daintily hemmed handkerchief from her sleeve and dabs her eyes. As Jenny puts her arm around her and gently rubs her hand, Ethel is touched by her warmth and her tears flow freely down her face.

By the time Cathy returns with the tea, her mother's grief is subsiding. Russell jumps up and clears a space on the table.

"There you are, Mrs Weedon."

"Call me Cathy, please."

"Thanks… for the tea. I knew it must be on its way, sooner or later. In the States we have the cavalry. You guys are just so different, you know, but underneath everything I guess we're pretty much the same."

Ethel looks up at them.

"I'll get some biscuits", she says, struggling to her feet.

"No, that's OK, I'll go. We can't have the birthday girl running about after us. This is your day, after all."

As he brings in a large plastic box containing several opened packets of biscuits, Ethel has regained her composure. She touches Russell on the hand as he reaches to put a small plate of chocolate Digestive on the table beside her.

"I'm sorry, dear," she says. "Please forgive me. I'm just a miserable old sod who needs constant attention."

"You deserve it," says Russell.

"Now don't be a creep, Russell, just when I'm beginning to like you. Cathy's right, you know. Dear Stanley would have been proud. He was a good man, and I seldom told him so. I'm sad for him now because he always felt that he could never quite match up to my first husband."

"Gran! I didn't know you were marr…"

"Mum! What are you saying? You've never told me this! Why would you keep it from me?"

"It wasn't your business, dear. I wanted our lives to be simple."

"Well who was this man?" says Cathy, her voice quivering.

"He was wonderful. I fell in love with him towards the end of the war. He was a real man, every inch a gentleman, and so handsome!"

"Mum! You mean poor Dad had to live in this guy's shadow? Please tell me you're making this up."

"You think I'm doolally?"

"No, but…"

"Wishful thinking, dear. I remember that man so clearly…it makes me blush to think of him, even now, all these years later. He was a pilot. A big man with a big heart."

"Gran! You old devil!"

"American, he was."

"You married an American!" Jenny screeches with laughter.

Russell is getting restless, unsure of the implications.

"Man, this is so weird."

"How can you have clung on to this secret for a whole lifetime and now suddenly decide to tell a total stranger, Mum? I can't believe this!"

"It's time," says Ethel, 'That's all, Cathy, it's finally time."

"What happened, Mrs Wood?"

"We were wed after the war... and so happy. Our plan was to move to Montana and have a family, but... John was flying one of their fighters back to The States when it had engine failure and came down in the sea."

A pause. They look at Ethel and realize the sadness she has had to deal with over a lifetime.

"The thing is," she says, "it was my birthday. He told me he was going to bring me the best present I'd ever had, but I never saw him again."

Ethel's tears overwhelm her, not just tears of sadness but of relief. So many years of pent up emotion had hardened Ethel Wood, and now for the first time her family were seeing her true self and making sense of their lives.

Cathy holds her mother in a close, forgiving embrace. "I love you, Mum," she says.

Russell smiles. "This is like a Doctor Phil showcase, guys... unbelievable! You're a brave woman, Mrs Wood, and you have an amazing family."

"Let's give her our present, Russell."

He goes over to the pile of one and picks it up. Ethel slowly tears the wrapping paper off.

"There was a time when I would save the paper," she says, "but as I told you, it's time!"

She finally discloses a set of champagne glasses.

"Ooh, I say."

"They're for drinking a toast, Gran," says Jenny. "Russell and I are getting married!"

A hesitant pause as the news sinks in. Then Ethel's face suddenly splits into a wide grin.

"Absolutely marvellous!" she coos, "the best present

I've ever had!"

"I'll get the champagne!" says Cathy as she skips out to the fridge.

AUTHOR BIOGRAPHIES

Chris – has been writing for about 25 years. Mostly short stories, flash fiction, and some poetry, as well as quite a few published articles. He also has one unpublished novel, now approaching its 3rd or 4th major revision after 15 years. His favourite writers are generally those who are the most dextrous with wit, wordplay and/or originality, and range from Jane Austen via Oscar Wilde and Saki to the modern day mistresses of prose such as Jane Gardam and Kate Atkinson.

Christine – moved to rural Normandy over twenty years ago. How she ended up there is a long story but the change added a rich vein of variety to her teaching career, her writing and life generally. She's had stories published in Scribble Magazine and anthologies such as WriteFrance, Sunpenny and Leaf Books. Her articles have appeared in The Lady, France Magazine, Countryside Tales and Writers Abroad. The culture shock has long ago worn off and she writes about anything that stirs her interest and her curiosity. The result is more or less evenly distributed amongst fiction and non-fiction with roughly twenty short stories and twenty articles so far published in magazines, anthologies, online or placed in competitions.

Geoff - is a writer/dabbler/blatherer who enjoyed eleven years in the Alpha family before wrenching himself away to live in a heavenly, muse-inducing writer's paradise beside a majestic river in Thailand, surrounded by palm trees, butterflies, monks and squirrels... and has written nothing ever since. After 25 years of working and travelling in the Middle East, culminating in two years of scribbling Alpha stories in a rickety cabin behind barbed wire in Iraq, it's time to set up a stained glass workshop on a firefly river bank and delve more deeply into a passion for photography.

Margaret - While delving into her family history, Margaret found two well-known writers – a playwright and a children's author – on her mother's side of the family. She wasn't surprised. Writing had always been as natural to her as breathing so she'd always guessed it was 'in her genes'. Margaret had her first success at the age of 11 when she won a box of chocolates in a school novel writing competition. After leaving school she trained to become a newspaper journalist and then worked as a freelance editor and writer. Since starting to write fiction in 1995, her short stories have appeared in magazines in the UK, Australia and Sweden, and in anthologies and small press publications. She has also won prizes in many international short story competitions. Find out more about Margaret at www.margaretskipworth.com

Morgen - has written all her life but only decided to get 'stuff out there' eighteen months ago. She likes to concentrate on short stories but since being an Alpha member, she has relished 'being prodded' by the regular writing challenges and these encourage members to get well and truly out of their comfort zones. Sometimes members are asked to get well and truly off the planet! This thinking outside the box has encouraged Morgen to dabble in extraneous areas including poetry and novel writing. Since 'coming out of the closet' she has had four short stories published, been nominated for a Write Well Award and been shortlisted in a writing competition.

Olaf – is basically a scientist with a background of mathematics and logic. He started working as a programmer on the word's first production computer and this coloured his professional life, which included university teaching. In retirement, he turned to writing as a relaxation, and led a writers' group as there was no-one else willing. He wrote some 70 short stories and some non-fiction articles, poems, two novellas and a full rewrite of The Ancient Mariner on a contemporary theme. It was a natural consequence that he should found Alpha Writers in 2004, and he rates this as one of his most satisfying achievements. He still writes for the village newsletter (now over 150 contributions), and feels that the value of writing without payment for local and specialised publications is totally underrated.

Rose – is a Canadian born ESL Teacher currently living and working abroad. An avid fan of the written word and writing, Alpha membership is definitely a hobby she enjoys immensely.

Rosemary - writes because she has to. You could take almost anything away from her except her pen and paper. Failing to stop after the book that everyone has in them, she has gone on to publish books in both non-fiction and fiction, the latter including novels, humour, short stories and poetry. She also regularly produces magazine articles in a number of areas and writes regularly for the dog press. She spends her life discussing her plots with the characters in her head and her faithful dogs, who always put the opposing arguments when there are choices to be made. She lives in North Yorkshire, with her husband and four dogs. For more details about the author please visit her website at www.rjkind.co.uk For more details about her dog then you're better visiting www.alfiedog.me.uk

Sally - works as a gardener and garden writer by day, with articles published in national and international newspapers, magazines and websites. By night (or at least, in what remaining free time she has in between looking after two teenagers plus assorted animals and a very unruly garden) she tries her hand at a little creative writing, which she finds a lot more challenging. So far she's had modest success, shortlisted for one competition in Writing Magazine, and coming second, with this story, in another WM competition. The best-selling novel – she hopes – is still to come.

Stephen - is someone who has always written for enjoyment which has over the years eased the pain of non-recognition. His early work for his school magazine still awaits discovery by a wider readership. A mischievous streak caused him to resign editorship of the parish magazine when he announced that the ladies of the gardening club would be holding a pant sale. Now continuing to write for pleasure rather than reward, he is concentrating on his first novel, a story of the Dogger folk who lived on land now beneath the English Channel.

Sue – is a school cleaner and a midday assistant. She joined Alpha when Olaf put a call out for members all those years ago. She admits she hasn't done much in the way of writing apart from entering a few competitions. However, in 2014 she had a small run on having letters published, including one in the Daily Mail, complete with photograph, on the joy of Buddleias. This year she's had a letter published (payment received) in a TV magazine, and she's made a pledge with herself to enter at least one competition a month. She's currently, very slowly, completing a Writers' Bureau Creative Writing course.

Suzanne - Originally from Derbyshire, Suzanne embarked on a new life in France in June 2009. She had a variety of jobs in the UK, including working in property, teaching German and French and finally a position as a library assistant (not as peaceful an environment as you might think). She lives with her husband and a largely unplanned family of rescue cats. Having lived for 6 years at an altitude of 1200 metres in the Massif Central, she recently moved in order to be closer to civilisation. She has had a few features published in French lifestyle magazines, Mslexia and Your Cat. As well as writing, Suzanne enjoys being outdoors as much as possible.

Zena - lives in Hertfordshire and was a historical researcher and writer until easing into semi-retirement recently. She now pours her creative energy into other avenues (unafraid of mixing metaphors), so with articles published, websites edited and a novel awaiting accolades, she looks forward to avoiding any form of work that requires being answerable. Don't you just love writing?

OTHER BOOKS BY ALPHA WRITERS

A Flower for Skalla
The City has become a bleak place since the Patreen invasion. Patreen stewards patrol the streets, while the original inhabitants, the Nasoots, are forced into exile or live as outlaws in the labyrinthine tunnels under the City. Only a handful of Nasoots remain in the City, where their superior technological skills are required by the Patreens. When the Nasoots invent a humoid far superior to the standard android, their plans to liberate the City from Patreen dominance take off with surprising results. Skalla, a young Nasoot girl, sparks the liberation as she gradually discovers things that were outlawed in the oppressive City.

This is a collaborative writing project from Alpha Writers Group – a science fiction story where each writer developed a new and exciting twist in the evolving plot.

Birth, Music, Sonnets
A collection of short stories and poems

Say n'more
Dora Finnucane, a one-time Eurovision Song Contest winner, has retired to a small village in the English countryside. All is not what it seems and when Lady Framworth is murdered, Dora finds herself embroiled in some dramatic events as the peaceful village becomes the hub of a sinister plot hatched by ruthless speculators.

'Say n' more' is a collaborative writing project from Alpha Writers Group – it is a crime novella in which each section ends with a telephone connection.

Find out more about Alpha Writers at:
http://alphawriters.net/

Alfie Dog Fiction

Taking your imagination for a walk

For hundreds of short stories, collections and novels visit our website at
www.alfiedog.com

Join us on Facebook
http://www.facebook.com/AlfieDogLimited

Printed in Great Britain
by Amazon